# fire in the valley

Printed in the United States of America

ISBN 978-1481137294

First Printing, 2012

dakota.lafontaine@gmail.com

# 1

A small fragment of the ceiling fell about six feet to her left, the century-old plaster shattering and raining hot shrapnel upon her exposed thigh. Another smaller piece soon followed, this time much closer. It met the ground with a sound that was barely perceptible against the background music, an opus performed by an orchestra of waist-high flames.

The falling ceiling made it real. All of it: her surroundings, the surreal nature of the past few weeks, and the immediacy of the danger that she now found herself in. Her heart quickened, and her vision began to lose focus. She began to feel faint as she looked longingly at the room's exit, but shut her eyes tightly and turned away. Sweat poured down her bare chest, and the reflection of the orange flames upon it bent as it rose and fell with her rapid breath.

*"How did I end up here?"* she wondered. She didn't mean this literally, of course; she could meticulously and carefully explain in painstaking detail the series of events and decisions that had recently transformed her relatively run-of-the-mill existence into a veritable real-life soap opera. By this question she rather meant, *"how did this bored and boring girl end up in a burning building by her own free will?"*

How had things spiraled so out of control?

Despite the panic that fueled her racing heart like the gasoline fueled the fires around her, she cherished every moment of the last few weeks like she had cherished nothing before, and knew that she wouldn't change a single thing even if she had the power to do so.

# 2

Bennett cleared his throat.

Melissa looked up from her screen and smiled up at him. He saw the blank document before her, and the two exchanged smiles that danced between amusement and frustration. Another day without drama—good news for most, but a death rattle for a failing newspaper.

Bennett sighed and pointed to a crumpled newspaper—a competitor's paper—in his hand. "I'm trying to do a crossword here. A little help?"

"What's the clue?" she asked, leaning back in her chair.

Bennett picked the glasses up from around his neck and placed them on the end of his nose, squinting as he looked at the page.

"Waste of space, eight letters."

"Newspaper," Melissa quipped, smiling smugly at her own cleverness.

Bennett threw the paper down on her desk playfully. "Newspaper's nine letters. Thank god you get paid for words, not numbers."

Melissa shot Bennett an annoyed look and threw the paper at him as he lumbered away. She got up from her chair and turned to the window behind her. A once great view had slowly disintegrated with time and economic downturn, but there was still a majestic nostalgia to it. Melissa could still remember that view—the one that kept her in this town, for better or worse.

The courthouse was the focal point as she gazed through the slightly dirty pane. The running joke had always been that the Washington Valley Caller was the town's superhero, its gaze always downward upon the evil crooks, gangsters and corrupt politicians that would presumably congregate in the courthouse. The paper had obviously seen better days, Melissa thought as she watched a vagrant slump against the side of the building below. What had once been a writing staff of ten was now comprised of Melissa, another writer named Henry, a tech, and her boss, Dave Bennett. The ever-present parade of associated press articles was punctuated only by the occasional teacher write-up about that week's school bake sale. The weekly periodical's content had become very weak as of late.

Melissa knew she still had the fire though, even if the leads that filled her inbox had less to do with political scandals or extraordinary conspiracies and more to do with the typical run-of-the-mill small city bullshit. There's only so many ways to write about unimportant legislation without using up all of the available adjectives. Yeah, she was in a rut, but she knew that with the way the traditional print paper was dying, she was lucky enough to be employed.

She saw her reflection in the glass. Despite having just turned thirty-three, she still had the look of a woman ten years younger. Her mother had once described her as "petite without being mousy," and seeing herself in the window, she understood what she meant. She looked at her own waist, breasts, and neck. In the semi-transparent image, her reddish-blonde hair looked fiery. She locked eyes with herself and sighed.

Bennett's tap on her shoulder quickly startled her away from her depressing self-assessment.

"Your sister called me again. She wants to talk to you. On my phone. Because you're ignoring her on yours."

Melissa made a sad face and clasped her hands together in mock prayer. "Please, tell her I'm not here."

Bennett shook his head.

Melissa quickly shifted tactics. "What do you have on your desk? I'll run out and cover it. Promise!"

Bennett shot her a disappointed look. "Seriously? She just needs to talk to someone."

Melissa smiled. "Please, feel free to!"

"I got a call in on a fire down at the WV Mall. Why don't you go down there for me?"

She looked at him cock-eyed. "When did that come in?"

"About twenty minutes ago. No deaths, no injuries. And my favorite Chinese restaurant still stands. Cops and fire crew ain't going anywhere, so I'm dragging my feet. It's yours. If you hurry, you'll catch the actual fire."

Melissa had her coat on before he was even finished. She kissed his cheek, mouthed "thank you," and was out the door before Bennett even had a chance to get back to his squeaky, burdened chair.

Right now, anything was better than being on Terry-Time. Even if it was something as mundane as interviewing a bunch of Washington Valley cops who were only marginally less bored than the Washington Valley reporters.

# 3

As Melissa settled into the driver's side seat of her Honda Civic, she couldn't help but sigh at the bullet she had just dodged. Terry-Time was her own little nickname for the almost-daily routine that involved her sister calling her and crying about her shitty love life. It didn't matter to Terry that Melissa's only love life over the last few months was with a little blue rabbit she kept in a shoebox under her bed. Melissa was by no means jealous of the never-ending revolving door of Terry's terrible boyfriends—better to be single than deal with those dolts—but Melissa wished her sister would at least realize that constantly hearing about this was getting to be a bit much. No such luck.

Melissa looked in her rearview mirror and saw the old cardboard box that sat behind her seat, a small layer of dust settled atop of its contents. It contained reminders of her last relationship, almost six months ago at this point. The asshole's name was Jonathan. He had been a waste of four months, a lying drunk who was considerably more interested in his nightly twelve pack than in making her happy. The box contained a few things she had left in his house that he had dramatically placed on the steps of her apartment building—a display so ridiculous that the whole complex knew her business by the time he'd finished. She'd hurriedly thrown it in the back of her car when he was long gone and now it just sat there, in the back of her car, a testament more to her laziness than her sentimentality.

With a sigh, Melissa turned the car on and began to back out of the parking spot.

# 4

"You've got to be kidding me," she mumbled to herself.

As Melissa's Civic turned the corner, she hoped to be greeted with a flamboyant wall of flames being furiously fought by a cavalry of courageous firefighters. Instead, she was greeted with the burned-out shell of a loading dock behind the town mall, a good deal of wet soot, and six or seven firefighters standing around, conversing with all the urgency of men who were discussing the past weekend's sports events. She sighed and pulled into a parking space. Despite years of covering the same mundane middle-America minutia, she somehow retained some small amount of naive optimism. A tiny piece of her was surprised to turn the corner and see that not only had the fire been a minor one that had been easily and quickly extinguished—not only had it only victimized a tiny area behind a mall—but she missed what little excitement there had been.

As she crossed the parking lot towards a sparse group of firefighters and curious bystanders, she rewound her handheld cassette recorder to its beginning. She often found herself slightly embarrassed while interviewing people; in the digital age, the paper had not found it in their budget to provide her with a modern recording device. She sometimes found herself thinking that her interviewees' eyes focused upon the bulky contraption and—seeing its age and quality—failed to take either she or the paper seriously. However, she was unsure how much of this impression was legitimate, and how much was in fact innocent, natural eye movement that her paranoia converted into perceived judgment.

She took a second to mentally confirm that she was about to record over an old, unimportant cassette, and began to scan the group for her mark. She recognized a few of the firefighters from past incidents and bake sales.

Her eyes fixed upon a heavyset, fifty-something Valley Fire Co. veteran named Dave—or was it Dan? Dammit, she had met him at least a dozen times; she should remember his name.

Wait a minute—who's this?

Directly to Dave-Dan's right stood a younger, strikingly handsome firefighter whom she had never met. She walked up to Dave-Dan, who was mid-conversation, all the while keeping her focus firmly fixed upon the stranger's deep brown eyes. Melissa loved eyes. As she came closer, she forced herself to peel her attention from the stranger and peered discretely at the name tags. Dan Harris—it *was* Dan—and the handsome stranger was apparently Shaun Duchane. She politely waited for a lull in the conversation, as none of the men acknowledged her arrival. After a few moments, she cleared her throat.

Dan smiled. "Hello Mrs. Bloome," he said, not even looking in her direction. He carried himself with the wit and pace of a jovial grandfather, constantly feigning boredom in an endearing way. Melissa found it hard to envision him moving quickly or with any purpose, let alone carrying someone out of a burning building.

"Hi Dan." She put her hand out to shake the stranger's. "It's *Miss* Bloome, actually," she continued, cringing as she immediately realized how flirtatious she had just sounded. Dan opened his eyes widely. She had hoped the embarrassing comment would be able to go unnoticed, but Dan certainly made sure that this was not to be. With this, he chuckled and wandered off to speak with two other firefighters, leaving the two alone.

"Hello, Miss Bloome," said Shaun, kind enough not to accentuate the "miss" and further acknowledge her comment.

"You're new?" Melissa asked.

"Yeah," he replied, momentarily distracted by a sound coming from the site where the fire had damaged the mall. When he confirmed that the source of the sound was his colleagues prying a wooden window frame away from the bricks which held it, he returned his attention back to the woman before him. "Yes. I started in May, but I've been fighting fires for about six years down in Decatur."

"Oh—are you from down that way?" Melissa asked.

"Kind of. I'm actually from right around here, but moved around a lot over the past few years."

Melissa waited for a moment, thinking that he would offer more information—like how he ended up in this town, thousands of miles from his birthplace—and then remembered that she was at work. "Uh," she said, as she fumbled with her tape recorder for a moment.

Shaun was tall, with light hair and eyes so brown that they looked black. He had about him a classic handsomeness; the type that would be as striking in the 1940's as it is today. He had a dimple in his chin and thin, serious lips. Despite the abundance of fire gear that he wore, Melissa could tell that he was in great shape; she could see the trails of his muscular chest and shoulders terminate into the lines of his exposed neck.

She snapped out of it and looked back up to his face. "Can I ask you a few questions about the fire?"

Dan came back, waving his hand impatiently, as if to shoo Shaun away. "I got it, I got it," he said, "go help Mike and Mike, only I get to speak to the pretty girls." He winked at Melissa, who smiled, partly humoring the old man and partly genuinely amused. She turned to Shaun to say goodbye, but found that he had already departed.

The creatively named Washington Valley Mall was a sizable two-story indoor shopping center that was opened in 1986. It acted as the town's heart; it was a meeting place, the core of teen social life, and its circular center (called *the Pavilion*) the default location for cutesy town events. She had never been behind the mall before, and found a series of loading docks, discarded wooden pallets, and broken, crooked blacktop that hadn't been maintained nearly as well as parking areas in the front. She felt as though she had stumbled onto a movie set; while the front of the mall was lavish and well-maintained, the back was stark and functional.

Through her interview with Dan, Melissa discovered that the old brick structure that had caught fire was a loading dock that led up to a hallway which connected the mall's small food court with a series of first-floor stores. The hallway was situated directly between the food court and stores, with a view of the scuffed white back entrances to a Chinese restaurant and an empty store that most recently housed a teen-oriented, "skater"-style clothing store.

The firefighters didn't know quite how the blaze had started, but were sure that it had originated in the hallway and spread to the loading dock. There, it had done quite a bit of damage, but had luckily stayed somewhat isolated. The mall was evacuated—a relatively easy task, given the fact that it was about two o'clock on a Wednesday afternoon—and the fire hadn't reached the restaurants. The contents of the loading dock were burned, and the windows and their frames destroyed, but the dock itself was mostly brick. Despite being rendered black, it was possibly salvageable.

Dan went on for quite some time, his eyes shut and his hefty frame leaning back on his heels. All the while, Melissa nodded politely, and kept finding herself scanning the scene for Shaun. She began to lose herself in the memory of their encounter. First, she replayed the conversation in her mind, over-analyzing her every word. Her thoughts then drifted to the man himself. Was he married? Why didn't she look for a ring? The closer she had gotten to him, the more handsome he had seemed. Why hadn't she met him before; surely she had been to police and fire events since May. Hadn't she?

And then she found him. He was assisting two other men in sifting through rubble, most likely the "Mike and Mike" that Dan had mentioned. She watched him as he worked. He carried himself in an almost majestic manner; there was a subtle poetry in the way he moved, even when performing such a simple task. While it still retained a distinct masculine cadence, she could only describe him as demonstrating a calm elegance, as though his every action was purposeful and calculated.

He was beautiful to behold.

As she watched, Shaun looked up from the pile before him. She quickly turned her head more towards Dan, but kept her eyes fixed on Shaun. From this distance, he surely wouldn't be able to tell. As Melissa watched, Shaun scanned the area where she stood, and seemed to stop when his eyes found her.

Her chest filled with a warmth that began to produce a girlish smile, which she fought so as not to seem too obvious. After a few moments, she began to second-guess herself; was he looking at her, or just looking in her direction? She took a deep breath, gathered some courage, and turned her head towards him so that he'd make no mistake that she was looking at him. When she did, his gaze quickly broke away—too quickly, the deliberate and obvious action of a man caught in the act.

This time, Melissa couldn't control the smile.

She turned back to Dan. As if on cue, he wrapped up his speech, and contentedly patted his rotund belly. "Yep," he said, "that's about the long and short of it." When Melissa stopped the tape, Dan added, "Off the record, hon,

10

it's too bad the fire didn't make it to that Chinese place. Brutal food." He stuck his tongue out to further convey his disgust, and slowly sauntered off towards the others, shaking his head. "Get to work," he joked to two nearby firefighters, "the city doesn't pay you to stand around being ugly!"

Melissa was looking down at the recorder, trying to see how much tape she had used, when she heard footsteps approaching her rear. "Hey there." She looked up at the horizon, frozen. It was Shaun. She quickly composed herself and turned around. "'Hey' yourself. Want to make a comment? I won't tell Dan."

Shaun laughed quietly and smiled shyly. "No, I'm all set. With how long that took, I have the feeling Sgt. Harris covered everything." He *had* been watching, she thought. Shaun took his hat off and rubbed his hair. It was short, well groomed, and almost perfect, despite being under a heavy firefighter's helmet for hours. Looking into the distance, he continued, "I guess you live in the area." He phrased it as though it were a statement, rather than a question.

"You guessed right," said Melissa. She was secretly pleased with herself. She was usually considerably less engaging and playful, and yet she found herself coming off comfortably flirtatious. The exchange felt like one that might take place in a film, and she felt good about her contribution to the romantic comedy playing out before her. With this, she overthought it, and suddenly became nervous. She decided not to push it. "I live down by Wright Street," she said.

"Ah." After a brief moment of silence, during which Shaun kept his hand on his head and nodded at the horizon, Melissa felt—no, she was *certain*—

that she was about to be asked out. Her stomach and posture tightened, and she felt as though she were about to have a bandage pulled off.

Instead, Shaun looked her in the eye, said, "Well, I hope to see you around again," and began to walk away. He put his helmet back on, and she said nothing. After about ten paces, he turned around and continued walking backwards. He put his hands into the air and gestured to the commotion around them. He smiled and added, "Under better circumstances."

# 5

Melissa's head was still spinning as she pulled her car into her apartment's parking lot. Shaun Duchane had weaseled his way into her thoughts, whether she liked it or not. As she exited her car and locked the door, she could tell her body was still a little tense from their conversation. That tension wasn't going anywhere, unless Shaun showed up and swept her off her feet, or if she used her...imagination. Melissa reached the entrance to the building and dramatically, but delicately, hit her head against the door. "Get out of your head, Bloome", she whispered, but that was easier to say than do.

Worse, it was time to open the door to her tiny apartment and call her sister. But first, she'd need a glass of Pinot Grigio to give her the energy to deal with whatever ridiculous drama Terry would soon drop into her lap.

Melissa entered the apartment and quickly took in her surroundings. The space was small, but she lived sparsely, which gave it a much larger feel. She quickly turned the lights on and poured herself a glass of the long sought-after wine. She lit a candle—harvest apples, her favorite scent—and plugged her cell phone into its charger. She took a deep breath and pressed the number "2", the speed dial for her sister.

The call connected, but she was met only with silence.

"Hey there", she said, forcing a smile she hoped would seem sincere over the phone. "I'm sorry I missed you earlier. How ya doing?"

A sniffle was followed by the reply, "I'm doing alright. Mom's just being a little overbearing, you know? The whole thing is just really frustrating."

Melissa and Terry's mother had fallen ill two summers ago, and required a good deal of attention. The duo could handle that. However, she was often difficult and—to put it gently—ungrateful for their continued care. A few months ago, Melissa and her mother had a bit of a falling out and haven't spoken since. While it barely clearly bothered her mother, it was tearing Melissa apart. As a way of protecting herself from having to face the emotions that her mother brought upon her, she went out of her way to seem particularly cavalier when speaking about her mother with Terry.

"I know hon, it's really hard,"—sip of wine—"but you need to realize how she is and just learn to patronize her a bit. It's an art."

"Well, I mean, that only worked for you up to a point..."

Melissa rolled her eyes and looked over to the candle. The light flickered off the walls and a fleeting thought crossed her mind: what if she accidentally knocked it over? The cheap Ikea shelf it sat upon was obviously flammable. What if it just came loose from the wall and sparked to life as the candle shattered on the floor? She imagined the orange-hot droplets of crystalline wax through the air. A delicate, private ballet of destruction playing out before her eyes. Maybe Shaun would be the one to come and rescue her, pulling her out of the flaming building just in the nick of time. She could

13

blame it on the glass of wine and the long hours at the paper. She was careless and fell asleep. Thank god he was so quick to respond.

Just as that thought passed, the crying on the other end of the call brought her back.

It was a silly thought anyway. With her luck, Dan and his heaving girth would be the one to drag her out of the fire. Slung over his shoulder, she'd likely get a front-row perspective of his jiggling, hairy belly, instead of the stomach of his younger protégé. She imagined being carried, upside-down, and sneakily lifting Shaun's shirt to see his sweat-laden and tense abs as he rushed her to safety.

No, with her luck she'd get Dan, and probably have to save *him*. Dammit, why didn't Shaun ask her for her number?

"Melissa, are you there?"

"Sorry, sorry, I'm here", she said, startled from her continued daydreaming. She really hadn't felt this way about someone in a long time, especially about someone she didn't even know and who was probably already married. "I just zoned out for a sec there. It's been a long day."

"You want to talk about it?" Terry asked, somewhat to Melissa's surprise.

"No, but thank you." She paused. "Would it be okay if I called you tomorrow? I'm feeling a little out of it."

"Of course," Terry said." Just make sure you call!"

Melissa hung up the phone and quickly downed what was left of her wine. She crossed over to the candle and blew it out, a strong whiff of artificial apples tantalizing her nostrils as the smoke swirled around her face.

*"There would be no fire tonight,"* she thought, as she made her way to the bedroom. But that didn't mean she couldn't dream about it.

# 6

A week had passed since the fire, and life trudged along at its usual pace. Melissa found herself spending most of her days staring thoughtlessly out the window at the courthouse, twirling a pen in her right hand and occasionally punctuating these lulls with furious bursts of caffeine-fueled work.

These bursts were Melissa's style lately. She would do nothing for hours, and then attack an article with insane ferocity, typing as fast as she could. These bursts were so productive that, by the end of the day, she had usually produced as much work as she would have had she worked all day at a reasonable pace. It was miserable, but it worked. She had operated this way for years now, ever since much of the passion had fallen out of her daily routine at the paper. When she first started out as a journalist—and even as recently as her start at the Caller—her days would seem to fly by. She'd write at a comfortable pace, her desk awash in a sea of yellow post-it notes, their illegible scrawl evidence of the urgency of their conception. She would agonize for minutes over a simple, single word—wanting to inject just enough form and beauty into her prose that she could call it her own without risking the prying, fumbling hands of the editor.

That is to say, *when* they had an editor.

Now, free to her own accord, she truly ruled her domain with impunity, free to wield her pen as she sees fit, to inject as much wordplay and as many flourishes as she'd like. Of course, at the end, this would all be lost on an unappreciative public. But who can blame them? No one is looking for clever, poignant observations or an author's impassioned dance with the English language in an article about the opening of a new Laundromat.

Yes, this freedom would have been a dream just a few years ago, but now she would stare out the window, her mind a blank canvas, and occasionally look over at the clock to bargain with herself about her next burst.

*2:18. I'll start at 2:20.*

*Shit. It's 2:21. Missed it. Okay, 2:30. I'll start then.*

When the time would come around that she truly had to produce some copy, she'd furiously type away as though she were holding her breath while doing so. She'd get just enough work done to warrant another session of nothingness, and repeat the cycle. Miserable.

"Melissa!"

Alarmed, Melissa snapped out of her stupor and turned her head slightly to find Bennett standing over her. Her posture hadn't moved, and she realized that she was positioned facing the window in a form not unlike that of Rodin's *The Thinker*. She at first thought that Bennett had simply stood next to her and addressed her as loudly and rudely as possible. However, upon scanning the room and noticing the eyes of the other staff members, she came to realize that Bennett had most likely called her name several times before getting this close.

"Yeah," Melissa mumbled, still acclimating to the situation in which she found herself.

"Fire alarm at Maple Glen. Get on it." Melissa leaned back in her chair, about to break into her usual routine of quiet sighs and lethargically rise from her seat. Just then, however, two words leapt to the forefront of her mind: "Fire alarm."

*Fire.*

She slammed her hand onto the desk, retrieved a pen, and headed straight for the door—she had no antique tape recorder, or even a pad to accompany the pen.

On the way to the Maple Glen Retirement Community, Melissa began to think about Shaun. "Fantasize" is a bit of a strong word, but she certainly began to think of him with an air of idealism. She imagined him stationery and standing before the last backdrop she remembered, the burnt-out remains of a mall loading dock. She could see the muscles of his forearms twisting as he slowly hoisted a piece of the rubble onto his shoulder; his tight jaw flexing. Not the overstated superhero jaw you would see on the cover of a romance novel, but rather the angular, real, understated jaw of an unattainable high school crush. Despite herself, she imagined running her finger down his cheek, coming to rest in a field of mild stubble. She imagined how it would feel to begin unbuttoning his shirt.

A distant car horn distracted her for a moment. Afterward, her mind then went on a bit of a tangent, and she began to think about how romantic lore paints the picture of the heroic firefighter—a noble, fit, intelligent specimen of righteous masculinity—and how almost every firefighter she'd ever actually met completely defied this stereotype. Most had been overweight, unkempt, older, and mustachioed. Very much like Dan, actually.

She smiled at the thought of what a realistic fireman calendar would look like.

When she arrived at the retirement community, she found exactly what she had expected to find: a perfectly intact building surrounded by elderly people, milling about and waiting to be allowed back inside. Peppered within the crowd were firefighters, standing out in their bright yellow jackets. Melissa was scanning the scene as she pulled into the parking lot, trying to find Shaun, even before she was able to feasibly distinguish individuals from one another.

Melissa got out of the car and walked towards the crowd. She didn't bring her pen with her; she simply began walking and continued scanning. She didn't see Shaun, and began to snap out of her single-minded march. At first, she was concerned that people had noticed her walking around in a semi-stupor, but after confirming that no one was paying her any mind, she simply walked back to her car. People walked past and eyed Melissa's car curiously. She began sifting through the small storage area between her seats, unsure what she was looking for, and stopped, shut her eyes, and collected herself. Surely she wasn't this smitten—could she be this desperate? Did she need sex? Affection? Attention? Validation?

She picked up her pen and some loose pieces of paper and walked back into the mumbling human mass. The conversations around her told of confusion—it seemed as though many of the residents were unaware of the drama in which they were participants. Looking around, she was suddenly struck by the memory of a story that she had done years ago, when a frustrated family member (after failing to gain any traction with the Department of Health and Human Services) turned to the Caller to complain

18

about the conditions of this facility. Maple Glen was comprised of three distinct subsections. The first was "retirement," a wing that simply provided condominiums to the over-fifty-five crowd, and offered activities and on-site health care. Next, there was "assisted living," which was for those who were capable of living alone, but who were not fully able to take care of themselves. Nurses, physical therapy, and additional healthcare options were available here, if she remembered correctly. Lastly, there was "Constant Care," which was reserved for those who were convalescent or suffering from Alzheimer's or dementia. It occurred to Melissa that she was right now among the latter group; how scary and confusing such an event must be for them. Her heart sank, and, as though all journalistic instincts had fled from her, Melissa milled about the crowd, looking at the aging souls all more lost than she. She suddenly felt ashamed for having such petty problems.

A shockingly petite female firefighter walked out from the main entrance of the building, holding what appeared to be the charred remains of a small toaster oven. She placed it on the ground, ran a piece of chalk across the top, and walked over to talk to some people who looked to be administrators at the facility.

Far to her left, Melissa spotted a lone woman who, despite being a resident, seemed to be a bit younger and—based on her body language—a bit more coherent than some of the others. Melissa began to walk towards her, reaching instinctively for her recording device. When she realized that it wasn't there, she looked back to her pen and paper, and quickly prepared some soft questions with which to begin a dialogue.

But then she saw him.

About one hundred feet away, a steel side door was being held open by a broken cinder block. From this entryway, Shaun stepped out, axe in hand. He shielded his eyes from the sun and scanned the scene, apparently trying to find someone. As his gaze passed her, she felt a sudden chill. In the distance—approximately where she had first stood—a fellow firefighter waved. Shaun stopped scanning, nodded his head upwards, and held four fingers high in the air. The other firefighter nodded, gave a thumbs up, and walked away. Once the exchange had ended, Shaun shot a look directly at Melissa. He smiled and began walking towards her.

Despite her schoolgirl anticipation, she found herself relaxing and feeling strangely confident as he approached.

"Well, well," he said as he closed the distance. He gestured with a nod at the crowd assembled outside the building. "The excitement never ends, does it?"

"No sir," she replied, playfully adding, "I thought you wanted to see me under better circumstances."

He immediately quipped, "Well then, let's stop waiting for better circumstances to come to us." She was shocked by how quickly the conversation had shifted. "Are you asking me out?" Melissa asked. "I think I am," he responded. "How's Friday sound? Where do you like to eat?"

Her mind was racing. So much information. He was single. He was interested. He was still so handsome.

She put these thoughts on hold and said, "I'm easy to please. Do you have a preference?"

"Hmm. Not really. We can stick with the theme of barbecue," he said, gesturing to the crispy corpse of the toaster oven at their feet. She laughed, not sure if he was serious; she actually really did enjoy barbecue.

Buying into the game, Melissa retorted, "I know a great place to go for toast." Again, she found herself to be comfortable and witty when she was speaking with this guy. She liked herself more. From the distance, someone called Shaun. It was the man with whom he had played charades a few moments ago. He began to walk away, but ended with, "how about seven? We can go to Incheon. Or Jake's."

Apparently, Shaun wasn't kidding; Incheon was a Korean barbecue place, and Jake's Smokehouse was a Memphis-style joint that had just recently opened very close to her apartment.

"I've been wanting to check Jake's out. It's a date," Melissa said, thinking that its proximity to her apartment could come in handy if the night went well. Shaun smiled and continued walking away. After a moment, Melissa wandered back to her car.

She was back in the parking lot of the paper with the car shut off before she realized that she had returned with no story whatsoever—no interviews, no official reports, no accounts. She laughed out loud and then cursed. She waited a moment before going back upstairs, and tried to bask in the happiness of the exchange she had just had. Unfortunately, it was all still too fresh and surreal. Instead, she thought about how she'd have to piece a story together from the single clue given to her by the toasted toaster, and went back to work.

# 7

The pile of clothing that lay in a heap on Melissa's bed was beginning to overwhelm her. Amidst the countless pairs of jeans, sweaters, and skirts, there had to be something that made her look good, or, at the very least, *feminine.* She plunged into the clothing abyss and came out with a nice black cocktail dress. Too formal. She was going to eat barbecue for Christ's sake. She threw it back on the pile and turned to the full-length mirror that hung on the outside of her closet door. It was the first time she had looked into it in a while. She wasn't unfit by any means, but she could see fewer details than she remembered. Her stomach was flat, whereas she had always had a slight valley down the center, the vague suggestion of underlying muscles. She had always had somewhat bony hips, but now they seemed smoothed over, as though a painter had blended her legs with her sides. She stared for a moment at her breasts. All in all, she still liked how she looked. Shouldn't something look good on her?

Couldn't he at least have planned something where she could show off a nice dress? Didn't he know what something so casual meant to a woman? It now dawned on her how unsexy their plans were. Nothing screamed "take me home now" like the sauce from a baby back rib dripping down your chin and staining your shirt. Finally, she decided on a nice striped sweater she had bought at the Loft a few weeks back, and a pair of jeans that accentuated her figure just enough in all the right ways. She hoped the outfit would make him do a double take. That, and she didn't mind if the clothing smelled like a Memphis smokehouse.

Jake's was only a few blocks from her apartment, so she decided to walk. Yeah, it meant leaving a little earlier then she would have liked, but it was a nice fall twilight and she thought it may calm her nerves before the big date. The sky was a welcoming swirl of orange and pink, the leaves a wonderful wine red. Her breath was slightly visible as she exhaled and inhaled the fresh autumn air. She had a good feeling about tonight.

The startling vibration she felt in her purse brought her back down to earth. She pulled her iPhone out and took a look at the screen. She was greeted with the image of her sister's best attempt at a sincere smile.

"Jesus Christ." She forgot she was on Terry Time tonight. She knew what she had to do—she needed to pre-emptively take the conversation over. To launch an offensive attack.

"Hey Ter, guess who has a date tonight?" she said in a sing-song voice.

"Ohmygodohmygodohmygod". Terry screeched. "Tell. Me. All. About. Him!"

"Well…" she began, launching into the serendipitous events that would soon lead her to be making doe eyes across a platter of short ribs. In the back of her mind, she felt just the tiniest bit guilty for deflecting the conversation. She knew that Terry needed someone to talk to; she had always struggled with depression, and Melissa truly didn't mind having to be there for her. She was family, after all. But whenever their mother was discussed, the conversation would inevitably turn into a Molotov cocktail of overwhelming negativity. And that usually led to Melissa becoming the unsuspecting storefront window. Hence, "Terry-Time."

"…and that leads us to where we are now," she said.

Terry was quiet on the other end of the phone. Melissa braced herself for an onslaught of crying, as Terry would invariably compare Melissa's fortune with her own desolate love life. Instead, she was greeted with a whoop. "I'm so happy for you. After all that shit Jonathan made you put up with, I'm happy to see you getting something you've earned." She paused. "It really gives me some hope."

Melissa didn't know what to say, partly because it was really surprising to have Terry react the way she did, but also because she was now at Jake's and she'd caught sight of Shaun.

"I'm really glad to hear that, Ter. But I've gotta go. I'm here!"

"Love you! Good Luck!" Terry said, as the line went dead.

Melissa put the phone back into her purse and waved at Shaun. He looked good, wearing an untucked button-down shirt and a well-worn pair of Levi's jeans. He smiled and leaned back against his grey, beat-up Dodge Stratus, a car that—if Melissa wanted to be truthful—seemed really out of place for a firefighter to be driving. She wasn't sure exactly what he should be driving, but she thought that it should have been fire engine red and have a minimum speed of seventy-five miles per hour.

"Hello there, Ms. Bloome. You made me look mighty heroic in that article you wrote up on that fire." He smirked.

"Why Firefighter Duchane, are you inferring that I'm biased?"

At this point, Melissa was within arm's reach of him and wasn't sure what to do. Should she go in for the hug? Should he? Would they just shake hands or head right on in? He alleviated any kind of awkward situation by reaching out and pulling her in close for a hug. He smelled just slightly of aftershave. "Shall we go in?" he said. He held the door for her and the two entered.

The smell of pulled pork and braised short ribs hit like a punch to the stomach as they walked into the main room. The space was large, and had a relatively modern feel to it. The tables were long slabs of finished wood with butcher's paper as the tablecloths and paper towel rolls as the centerpieces, but the decor was relatively tasteful and didn't overwhelm you. The maitre'd led them into the main dining room. In fact, it was nicer than some of the restaurants she was used to frequenting, though that could also be a slight against the type of establishments she was used to. Really though, how many meat shacks did she know that even had a maitre'd?

As their table was being readied, Shaun leaned into her, his cheek almost touching hers. She could feel the prickles of his stubble. He whispered:

"I do realize in hindsight how awful of an idea it was to have our first date here. If we need to bail, let me know. Their backs are turned."

Melissa let out a small laugh and shook her head.

"We're committed now, officer. No turning back."

"I'm a firefighter, not an officer," he smiled.

The matire'd led them to the table and they sat, the butcher paper rustling as they lay their hands down upon the table top.

"That brings up a good point", Melissa said, half-seriously. "When I see a police officer, I know to call him officer. When I see firefighter, I have absolutely no idea what to call him. Is it firefighter? Is it fire officer? Maybe just beefcake?"

"Actually, we prefer Sultan Beefcake," he said, matter-of-factly. Melissa burst into a fit of laughter and almost choked on her drink. "Actually," Shaun continued once the outburst subsided, "I'm a Sergeant. So call me that."

"Unfortunately, that's not going to happen. Forever and ever, you're going to be Sultan Beefcake. And if you're a good boy, I may even add an 'esquire' to the end of that."

"M.D?" he volleyed back.

From there, the conversation came quickly and easily. Melissa found herself feeling less guarded and enjoying the conversation. She wasn't worrying about what or how she was eating, and there were no awkward moments of silence. They actually seemed to have legitimate chemistry. She was finding herself more and more excited as the night progressed. Could this really be happening? She was intoxicated by his charm, the noise of the patrons, and the smells of delicious food that wafted around her.

The time flew by and they both found themselves full and ready for the night to take them wherever it felt it wanted to. Shaun picked up the bill and paid. Normally, Melissa would have at least protested and tried to pay for her meal, but, in this case, she didn't argue. It just felt natural and protective. She was slightly drunk from the beer, so she let it slide. She just hoped that the night wasn't about to end.

"Well, this is my ride," he said, as they left Jake's. He paused in front of his Stratus and turned to her. "Can I give you a lift back home?"

Melissa shook her head. "It's a nice night, why don't you walk me home?"

Shaun smiled, nodded, and headed towards her. He reached for her hand confidently and she took it, hoping that he wouldn't notice the slight tremor within it.

The autumnal orange of the sky had given way to the blue-black night dotted with pinpricks of starlight. The trees swayed and rustled with a chill that the sun had stirred up with its setting. Shaun's hand let go of Melissa's, and she found his arm around her waist as he pulled her closer to him. They turned off of the route that she had taken to get to the restaurant, heading east.

"I grew up not far from this street, you know. Down a few blocks on Russet", he said, pointing into the oblivion of the night ahead. "I used to run up this block when I'd practice for football."

Melissa smiled and looked up at him. Of course this good old American boy played football growing up. It also gave her a nice little snapshot into his past. He continued, "I lived here until I was seventeen, and then we moved because my dad had to take care of my grandfather."

They walked in silence for a few moments, taking in quiet town and closed shops around them. "I'm not from around here", she said. "Came here for college, and stayed in the valley..."

"For love?" he asked.

"For love," she said, smiling bashfully. "But as time went on, the valley turned out to be a little more to my liking than the guy."

She looked off into the familiar darkness, and added, "it's home now."

As they turned off of Lincoln onto Alabaster, they found themselves staring at a construction zone. The street was entirely blocked off with sloppy temporary fencing, and a large dumpster stood behind it like a hulking monster incarcerated behind thin, flimsy bars. Melissa looked at Shaun, who was looking at the surrounding buildings. After a second, he smiled like a boy, tightened his grip on her hand, and said, "come on, I know a shortcut."

They walked into an alley, and approached the back entrance to a cluster of shops whose fronts faced Alabaster. Next to the illuminated door was a keyless magnetic square marked "FOR POLICE / FIRE USE ONLY." Shaun pulled a small plastic device out of his pocket. At first, Melissa thought it was a USB thumb drive like the ones they had at work, but she realized what it was as he waved it in front of the magnetic plate. A small red light turned green, followed by the dull ka-chunk of a lock being disarmed. With a boyish wink, Shaun walked through the door and said, "Key to the city." Giggling, Melissa followed him through a dark back corridor and towards a side entrance. She could smell pastries as they passed the back of Roeber's Bakery. As the duo pushed through the exit and again into the brisk night on the other side, Melissa asked, "won't you get in trouble for that?" Shaun laughed and said, "Everything is ten years behind here, they don't track anything." He nodded towards their original intended path, now on the other side of the construction, and they continued on their way. She brought herself closer to him.

They walked in contented silence until they reached her door. She was hoping that with each step, time would slow down. Unfortunately, it just seemed to speed up. Finally, there they were.

Melissa fumbled with the lock on her door. With the click of the latch, she turned and looked up at him. "Shaun, I had a..."

She was cut off by his mouth touching her own. A kiss sweet in nature but slightly aggressive. She liked it.

He pulled away and looked down at her. "I had a great time, Melissa. I hope I can see you again."

Melissa just looked at him, a toad in her throat. She found her voice— "I'd like that."

He smiled and began to turn, when her hand shot out and grabbed his. It took them both by surprise.

Her own bravery astounded her. "I do think, Sultan Beefcake," she said, her eyes staring into his, "that I'm not quite done with you."

Melissa led Shaun through the door. It closed behind them with a click— and with it, they both became aware that the night they thought was about to end was just beginning.

# 8

"I can't believe Valentine's Day is right around the corner."

Melissa rolled her eyes at Shaun. She held the cell phone to her ear with her left hand and doodled absent-mindedly with her right on a scrap of paper.

Terry continued. "But you don't really have to worry about that. I'm sure Captain Beefcake has something so incredible planned for you that I'll be jealous about for months."

"Actually, Terry, he's a Sultan." Shaun shot a surprised look at Melissa, which she quickly waved off. "And really, don't throw yourself a pity party right now. It's still early in the month. Why don't you go to one of those speed dating things? They have a ton of them this time of year."

Terry paused for a moment. "I don't know, that just seems so desperate."

"Terry, who cares? It's a good change of pace. It will get you out of the house." Melissa was starting to get agitated. "You may meet someone. And who cares if they seem desperate. There's nothing wrong with a good...you know...every now and again."

"Really? So sorry that not all of us can fall in the hands of heartthrobs every time you need to get some ass. It's called scruples. You might want to try and have them one time."

Melissa rubbed her temples, hoping it would calm her down. It didn't work as well as she would have hoped.

Terry continued. "I just wish something exciting would happen, to at least make me feel alive. I'm like a...a...sexless...zombie. And there you go, 'oh, look at me, with a great guy taking me out after talking with him for like, thirty seconds.'"

Melissa stifled a laugh. "Terry, I know you're a little emotional right now, but that really doesn't give you a free pass to act like a bitch to me."

*Click.*

Melissa wanted to throw the phone, but her hand was quickly held back by the realization that doing so would cost her more than $300. She set it on the coffee table in front of her and took a deep breath as she leafed through a cooking magazine that lay there.

Shaun walked over and sat next to her, placing a coffee mug full of red wine in front of her. "You know, you have the mouth of a sailor." He took a swig from his beer as she playfully swatted him with an issue of *Bon Appetite*. "And, apparently, you're just as violent."

Melissa laid her head in his lap and looked up at him. "You know, you're lucky not to have a sister as mental as mine is."

30

Shaun took another swig of his beer. "You know, I can hook her up with one of my co-workers, or better yet, one of the volunteers. They only joined to name drop that they're firefighters at bars for some easy ass anyway."

"God no! What if it actually worked out? She'd probably move here and I'd have to put up with her mood daily swings in person. Then I may become her. It will be like an episode of the Twilight Zone."

"I forget. Which one of you is the neurotic one?"

"Har har." Melissa turned over and focused her attention on the TV in front of her. The news was on, muted, showing a weatherman standing outside, sans coat. Children were playing baseball in the background. It looked like a beautiful spring day.

"It's crazy that the weather has stayed this hot. February should make me want to never leave the house, not contemplate going for a swim."

Shaun nodded in agreement. "It just means that March is going to be super brutally cold. Last thing you want before spring actually starts."

Melissa agreed. A silence fell over them. Shaun looked around and spoke up. "What's with you and all the candles? It's enough to make a firefighter lose sleep in here."

"I like them," Melissa said. Her response was a bit more solemn than the joking question seemed to warrant. She stared into one of the flames. "They..." she began. She looked over at Shaun, who was silent and listening intently. She felt pressured to finish the sentence, but didn't really have anything to say. "They just...it's like, here I am in this empty house. No pets, not even a mirror aside from the bedroom. Nothing moves except for me. And then here are these flames. These little...I don't know...constantly

31

performing these little dances. These reminders that there's some sort of life in this house. Some sort of force other than me."

The two looked at each other for a few moments as though a spell was cast upon them. After a moment, they both felt a bit awkward. Shaun began a sentence, but his voice was breathy. He cleared his throat and tried again. "That makes sense. I get that." After a second, he smiled, both acknowledging the strange air. "Want to see what's on TV?"

Melissa began flipping through the channels. Everything on was either reality TV or some spin-off of *Law & Order*. She knew she probably had better things to do, like actually write an article that was due tomorrow; however, she didn't have the motivation, especially because she knew only three people would probably read it anyway.

She handed the remote to Shaun and re-adjusted herself to look back up at him. He really was attractive, which still took her off-guard at times. She knew she wasn't bad looking herself, but it still excited her that somebody who could probably be in an actual hunky firefighter calendar was just as attracted to her as she was to him. Shaun looked down at her and smiled. She could feel his penis harden slightly under his jeans. She was more than a little game for that.

Melissa slid up and wrapped her arms around Shaun's neck, giving him little kisses, until finally, with the last one, she bit his lower lip and held it for a second before letting go.

He got the hint. He pulled her in close and began to kiss her neck. The kisses created an electric sensation on her bare skin. She playfully pulled on his ear with her teeth and whispered "I think you should take your pants off."

She was as comfortable and confident with him sexually as she was in conversation. In this way, too, she liked herself more when she was with him.

Shaun picked her up and threw her down on the couch. He fumbled with her belt—making him grunt quietly—which turned her on even more. She pulled her jeans down to her knees. He took care of the rest, pulling them off fully in one, quick motion. He slid his hands up her thighs and delicately pulled her panties down. He grabbed her legs, placing one on each shoulder. He was fast and determined and yet gentle. With a mission, he began to sink down—a hummingbird pursuing his nectar.

In between the moans of pleasure, Melissa's eyes caught sight of a candle on the night stand. The tongue of the flame mimicked the tongue of her lover. Despite Terry, her mother and the paper, life couldn't be better.

Melissa's phone rang again. She sighed and reached for it, fully expecting an apology from Terry. When she saw who was calling, however, her heart stopped and she went cold. It was her mother. She picked up but held the phone away from her ear for a second, staring at it as though it was an injured stranger that she didn't know how to help. She could hear her mother say her name, tinny and distant in the tiny earpiece.

It had been months since they last spoke, but that didn't stop her mother from picking a fight within minutes. Without moving from the couch, the next hour was a rollercoaster of screaming, cursing, accusations, and waiting for apologies each thought they deserved. Shaun sat silently next to Melissa, rubbing her back gently while she raged into the phone and stared, shaking, at the candle on the table that cowered from her whenever she made a large movement. The conversation finally ended in a stereotypical exchange of the word, "fine," stubbornly volleyed back and forth a few times before Melissa's mother finally hung up.

Immediately, Melissa broke into tears and fell into Shaun's arms. She unloaded months of tension and pain onto him, and he was like a dream. He held her and consoled her without judgment. When she calmed down a bit, he rubbed her feet and discussed the situation, remaining supportive without ever simply telling her what she wanted to hear. When she was finally feeling better, he ran to an all-night convenience store to pick up her favorite: vanilla ice cream and mini-pretzels. They sat up for hours, watched a movie, and held each other. When she fell asleep, Shaun carried her to bed, kissed her on the forehead, and turned out the light.

# 9

Melissa and Shaun had both stayed at either his or her place every night for the past week, and waking up together began to feel completely natural. The following Sunday, the two decided to wander out of Shaun's single-story rancher to go get coffee down at the *Bread Box*, a small bagel shop in a tiny strip of stores on Fay Street that served coffee and home-baked pastries. They walked in, and a quaint bell jingled as the door shut behind them.

They stood in line behind an elderly couple, reading the coffee menu. Having just come in from the cold, Melissa stayed close to Shaun, with one gloved hand wrapped around his waist. Before they could order, however, Shaun's phone rang. He pulled it from his pocket and said, "It's Dan about tomorrow." Melissa wasn't exactly sure what he meant; as far as she knew, tomorrow was supposed to be like any other Monday at the firehouse.

Nonetheless, Shaun walked off without saying a word, leaving the shop. Melissa watched as he stopped for a moment outside the door, and then began to pace; it was a common habit of his. Thinking very little of it, she turned her attention back to the menu.

After a moment, Shaun burst back into the shop, causing the Christmas bells attached to the door to clang boisterously and alert everyone inside as to the urgency of his entry. "We gotta go," Shaun said, his hand reaching out for hers. She instinctively reached out to him, expecting to be tugged out the door; however, despite his state, Shaun managed to take her hand gently.

"What?"

"We have to go. Now. Big fire down by 18th and McGonicle." They sped out the door, sending the bells—which had just finally calmed themselves—into another frenzy.

Shaun walked with unblinking, double-speed determination, and seemed to forget Melissa was even in tow. He pulled his keys out of his pocket, his scruffy jaw visibly tense, and got in the car. Melissa struggled to keep pace, but managed to get into the passenger's seat just as he turned the ignition. Under his breath, he whispered something unintelligible.

Melissa's head began to spin with questions. Are we going to the fire house? Is he dropping me off somewhere first? Why is he so upset? Given Shaun's state, she was too afraid to ask, and just stared through the road ahead of the car as it came at her. She would occasionally sneak a peek over at him, find him in the exact same trance-like state, and return her eyes to the road.

Finally, he spoke. "My place is on the way. You'll get out there." She nodded, and attempted to say "okay," but her throat only allowed air to emerge, coupled with the barely-perceptible noise of her dry lips parting.

Melissa felt like she was in a dream; never before had Shaun spoken to her with such coldness or authority. She felt vaguely offended, but, given the circumstances, felt sure that there was something more to this than she was aware of, and let it slide. 18th and McGonicle...that was easily one of the worst areas of the city.

Dropped off in front of Shaun's house without a word spoken, Melissa stood at the curb for a moment, staring across the street, in a bit of shock about the events that had just transpired. She began to worry about the fire and Shaun's safety—was his concern due to the severity of the blaze? She went into the house and called the paper to see if they knew anything about the fire.

Her first attempt rang eight times before the machine picked up. Sundays were usually a bit slow, and she'd be surprised anyone was actually at the office. Still, she had to try.

For a reason she couldn't explain, she tried again. This time, to her surprise, Bennett picked up. He seemed cavalier, which immediately put Melissa at ease about the severity of the fire. Bennett heard about the situation, but said that all accounts report the fire to be small and under control. Melissa thanked him and began to pull the phone away from her ear.

"Melissa? *Melissa?*" came the voice on the other end.

She brought the phone back to her jaw. "Yeah?"

"Thought you hung up," Bennett said. "Just got a text from Henry. Says there were injuries. Get down to the hospital and see what you can dig up."

Melissa was at the hospital in twenty minutes, attempting to figure out exactly where the injured had been taken. Bennett met her there and was speaking with some police officers in front of the emergency room. An hour later, she found herself speaking with a firefighter named Mike Gullio, whom she had never met. As far as he knew, the fire was in a private residence, owned by the grandmother of a known drug dealer named Manny Goza. The fire was the result of an explosion, and was mostly contained to one home. This was lucky, given that the house was one of a tightly-packed array of row homes. There were several victims, however. Goza himself was killed, as was an accomplice named Gabriel Hernandez. Three others were injured—all males in their twenties or thirties—and were all currently being treated in the small emergency room mini-suites directly next to the hallway where Melissa and Mike were having their conversation. Two of them were associates of the casualties, the third a man just walking past on his way home.

Mike was young, with olive skin, gelled hair, and the face of an overgrown altar boy. He seemed sweet, but, on occasion during their conversation, Melissa couldn't help but feel as though his eyes were lurking towards her chest whenever she'd glance down at her notepad. Twice she snapped her eyes back up at him, but either he was too quick or she was simply being paranoid. She thanked him for his time and, finding the door wide open, took a step to the first room.

Lying on his left side in a hospital bed was a heavily tattooed Hispanic man in his early twenties. His head was shaved, and he sported an angular, sharp, meticulously-trimmed moustache and beard. He was lean and muscular, shirtless, and being treated by a nurse who sat on a chair next to the bed. He didn't seem to be burned, but was having a very long and serious-looking cut stitched up his side, from his hip bone to above his right kidney. His eyes were elsewhere, and he didn't seem to be in pain; perhaps he was still coming to grips with the events to which he had just been witness, or the loss of his friends. Melissa wondered how he managed to be cut. Perhaps shrapnel from the explosion? In the corner of the room, behind the nurse, a very tall, burly police officer in a thick jacket stood watch, perhaps gearing up to take a statement after the young man's wounds were tended to.

Melissa moved to the next room and poked her head in. This time, the door was open, but only by a few inches. She looked inside to find a man strikingly similar in appearance to the first, sitting on a chair, wearing a hooded sweatshirt, and speaking with three police officers, who stood in a triangle around him. This man had no apparent injuries. After a moment, one of the officers noticed Melissa and nodded to her, as if he knew her. She looked back for a moment, and, unable ascertain any of their conversation, backed out and moved on to the third room.

As she was about to step inside, her cell phone rang. It was Shaun. She picked up. "Hey. How are you?" he asked. "Fine. I should be the one asking you. You terrified me back there. Is everything okay?"

"Yeah, yeah, totally. Everything's fine. Sorry about the frantic—you know, frantic-ness of the whole thing. Didn't mean to freak you out. I just had to get down to the scene. There have been some weird fires lately, and that area's really—lots of families close together. Where are you now?"

"Hospital, looking into some of the people involved. Know anything good?"

"Not really. Two dealers burned up, two of his main dudes are at county. Is that where you are?"

"Yeah."

"Yeah, they're there with you then. And some kid got a minor burn or two. Cops thought he was there trying to score drugs, but he says he was literally just walking by on his way home. Apparently there was a blast. We're trying to figure out what started it. It was intentional, though. We know that."

Melissa arched her back so she could see into the room. Sure enough, there sat a man in a chair, watching television, with fresh gauze wrapped around his right arm. He didn't seem to pay her any attention.

"Are you still there?" Melissa asked.

"Yeah."

"Will Dan let you go soon?"

"Probably. A few others who were on today are going to stick around and do some more clean-up."

"Okay, see you soon."

"Okay," Shaun said, and, after a pause, added, "sorry again about earlier."

Melissa delayed a second and hung up without acknowledging his apology. She wasn't sure why she did that—it was an uncharacteristically catty thing to do. Did she just want to punish him a tiny bit for scaring her?

From behind her came a voice. "Dan must be the boss man." Melissa turned around to find the man from the third room leaning against the wall directly behind her. He was young; under twenty-five by the looks of him. He had dark hair, piercing gray eyes, and a five o'clock shadow that came very close to being a short beard. He was clad in jeans, worn sneakers, and a plain black jacket. She looked behind him into the room to see if there was anyone else with him. There was no one. Her eyes found his again, and she found herself momentarily fixed upon them. They were still, unblinking, and so shockingly grey that they almost seemed white, like those of a Siberian Husky. After a moment, she refocused. She tried to read his expression—was he joking? His face, neutral, gave her no clues. He didn't smile, and yet didn't look fully serious; he just peered at her.

Finally, after failing to assess the man's intentions, she collected the indignation that she knew she was expected to express, and said, "Excuse me?"

"Dan must be *el jefe*. Or else his aging yet well-meaning father. Given the awkward end to the phone call, though..." He trailed off, and nodded his head a few times.

"Though what?" Melissa asked, equally intrigued and annoyed.

"Well, it just sort of trailed off. No final act. No curtains. Trouble in paradise? Or, perhaps you two are party to an illicit liaison?" As he completed the sentence, he gestured dramatically with his non-bandaged hand. His eyes simply didn't move at all. Melissa just watched him, struggling with (now sincere) indignation, confusion, amusement, and an array of other emotions that she couldn't quite pinpoint. "I, I..." she began, but didn't know where to go from there.

"I wouldn't have ended a conversation with you like that," he said. "Not because you're a beautiful woman, but just because of common courtesy. You know,"—and then he said the last three words with a hushed whisper, as though he were divulging a secret—"the social contract?"

A strange man, speaking in strange prose, saying strange things to a stranger, Melissa thought. "Right," she said, nodding sarcastically, "the social contract. Totally. By the way, speaking of the social contract, this," —she extended a finger, pointed at his chest, and then pointed at her own—"is very normal, just talking to a stranger like this."

The man pursed his lips and nodded. He didn't seem at all put off by the strangeness of the exchange. Melissa still didn't know what to think of him. After a moment of awkward-yet-mesmerizing eye contact with the stranger, she spoke up again, "Dan *is* the boss man. The *jefe*."

"Ahhh," the strange stranger smiled.

"Not that it's any of your business," she added. The man shut his eyes, shook his head slowly, and dramatically made a motion with his hands, as if to say he was washing his hands of the entire ordeal.

Melissa turned and looked down the hall; it was empty except for her. After a short moment of fear, given the fact that she was alone with this bizarre man, she remembered that she was one shriek away from commanding the attention of four police officers who stood in nearby adjacent rooms.

She turned her attention back to the man, her mind still processing the exchange. She was about to walk away, but continued to speak with him. "What exactly is your deal?" she asked in a hushed, accusatory tone.

"Just talking. Dialogue. Well, *mono*logue if you're not engaging me," said the man, who seemed to become more relaxed the more irritable Melissa became. She noticed what appeared to be an old burn scar on his left forearm, peeking out of his sleeve.

When Melissa cocked her head to the side, as if to say, "What the hell is wrong with this guy," he smiled, patted his hand on his stomach and said, "I'm sorry if I offended you. I'm just waiting for someone." Melissa relaxed,

41

and began to feel a bit silly for how tense she had become. He continued, "I just couldn't help but make a comment when you and your husband were ending your call."

"He's not my husband," she found herself saying. She was shocked by how quickly and bluntly the words came out of her. Why did she care what this weird guy thought? Why did she say it as though she were embarrassed by Shaun or the phone call?

Melissa could hear footsteps coming down the hall behind her, growing in volume as they approached. A moment later, a tall Hispanic man wearing a white t-shirt and sunglasses turned the corner, saw Melissa, and stopped. He nodded to the man with whom she spoke, as if to ask, "Is it okay to come in?" Her strange new friend made a very dismissive beckoning gesture.

"I know," he replied, turning his attention back to Melissa, "there's no ring on your finger. I just wanted to see how you'd react."

Melissa suddenly found herself far more taken aback than she had already been. Her whole body tensed up again as she processed the implications of this comment. "Wait—what?"

The man stopped leaning against the wall, pulled a small yellow sticky note out of his pocket, tore it in half, found a pen in another pocket, and scribbled on it. He folded it in half, tucked it between his fore- and middle fingers, and held it out to her. He said, "And based on your reaction, you might call me if you had my number. You also might not. But you certainly couldn't if you didn't have it. So all I'm doing here is expanding your options. Exposing another fork in the road."

Now standing directly in front of her, inches away, he stared her square in the eye with a confidence that she had never before experienced in her entire life. She found herself completely lost in his icy eyes; time seemed to slow down, and she became suddenly aware of the sounds of her heart and breathing. After what seemed like an hour, she reached out and took the piece of paper. Without smiling or blinking, the man nodded his head gently and walked out the door. The man in the white t-shirt delayed a moment. Before following his partner, he leaned in towards Melissa, cocked his head down, and, peering over his sunglasses, said, "It's good to have options." He smiled and disappeared. She truly felt as though a spell had been cast on her, and she stayed facing the wall where they had stood until their footsteps were lost in the distance.

She began to come back to reality, but her heart continued thumping loudly. She swallowed for the first time since the strange man appeared behind her. Her thighs tingled and felt cold.

About two minutes later, Bennett came into the room. She hadn't even heard him walk down the hallway. She shoved the paper in her pocket, and scrambled to decide what she would be expected to say if nothing strange had just happened. She came up with nothing, and, after a second, excused herself to the restroom.

There, she sat down on the closed toilet seat and pulled the piece of paper from her pocket.

Roman

555-8197

# 10

At no point after the strange encounter at the hospital did Melissa consider discarding the phone number. Every few hours, she would think about it and ask asked herself why she hadn't done so, but couldn't pinpoint an answer. Throwing it out just seemed wrong in a way that she couldn't explain, as though it was some keepsake of a cherished memory. After a day or so, she placed the piece of paper in a drawer and, for the most part, forgot about it entirely.

One week after the encounter, however, Melissa was sitting in her living room, curled up on a chair, and reading a book on her Kindle. She found herself suddenly panicked by the thought of Shaun finding the phone number. She headed into her bedroom and over to the drawer. She carefully opened it, and picked the piece of paper up, intending to throw it away. Instead, she looked at it for a moment, and decided instead to tear off the name, leaving only the number intact. After doing so, she realized that a phone number—nameless or not—could still arouse reasonable suspicion.

She briefly considered putting the number in her cell phone, but realized that doing so seemed even more risky.

Finally, Melissa picked up a pen, thought for a second, and— remembering a recent email exchange with her cousin Lana, who had recently purchased a new home—wrote "termite and radon inspector" above the number.

She stared at the paper, disgusted with herself; not due to the fact that she couldn't bring herself to discard another man's phone number, but rather due to the pathetic and transparent ruse that she was attempting to perpetrate. Not only would she have no need for such an inspector's services, but the number itself was clearly written in someone else's handwriting. Furthermore, the name and number were written with different pen color.

After a few moments, she shook her head. *Oh well.*

With the number at least somewhat disguised, she placed it back in the drawer, buried it under some supplies, and went back to her book.

The following Wednesday, after a particularly frustrating bout of Terry-Time, Melissa hung up the phone, squeezed it in her hand, and then took a deep breath. She could hear Shaun in the other room. She wandered over to Shaun and snuggled up next to him. He muted the television, put the remote control down next to him on the couch, and put his arm around her. He had heard enough of her conversation to know that there had been some tension, and kissed her forehead. Strangely, Melissa felt no sanctuary in his arms, kissed him absently, and got up. She moved first towards the bathroom, and then abruptly changed course and walked into the bedroom. Before even making a conscious decision to do so, she found herself standing over an open drawer, with the phone number in her hands.

*What the hell am I doing?*

She let the phone number go as though it suddenly burned her hands, and slammed the drawer shut. Her eyes darted towards the bedroom door, but Shaun was nowhere to be seen. Most likely he was still on the couch, awaiting her return. She held her breath and listened for a moment; she could hear that the television's sound was turned back on. She felt her eyes well up with tears, and paced back and forth, trying desperately to figure out what she was thinking, and why on earth she had felt as though this piece of paper could provide for her the relief that Shaun hadn't. She didn't understand this odd obsession. Was it that this piece of paper represented something strange and otherworldly, and therefore the possibility of some sort of escape from the frustrations that her sister brought into her life? She shook her head, coming to no conclusions, and walked back out to the living room, wiping her eyes.

The next night, she found herself looking at the phone number again. This time, though, she had done so consciously, carefully replaying the hospital exchange in her mind. She had just come home from work—she wasn't seeing Shaun that night—and walked into her bedroom. She hadn't even taken her shoes off, and had only tossed her purse and laptop onto the kitchen table. Her neck muscles tight with the tension of a hectic-yet-fruitless day of work, she stood over the open drawer, hovering as she had the night prior.

She replayed the conversation in her mind yet again, but this time, she altered the ending ever so slightly: when they stood, eye to eye—before taking the piece of paper—she brought herself in closer to Roman.

Now, looking down at the paper, Melissa sat down on the bed and allowed her eyes to rise. She looked over at the window, sat the paper down on the dresser, and lay down on the bed. Her eyes shut and she allowed herself to melt back into the scene at the hospital.

*She could feel the last diminishing tingle of the wintry cold leaving her fingertips and nose, a reminder of her walk from the car to the emergency ward. She could smell the vague scent of antiseptic. In her mind, she transformed it into a warmer, autumnal smell, like pumpkin pie. She turned the corner into the third room and stared into Roman's strange eyes.*

She relaxed on the bed. Her right hand found her right hip, which was peeking out from between her dress shirt and skirt. The very tip of the nail on her middle finger danced across it gently.

*She quickly looked down the hospital's hall and made sure that no one was coming. She leaned in, touched her nose to Romans, took her right hand, and ran it up his stomach to his chest. He was warm and more muscular than his loose jacket showed. Her hand sank down and wrapped around his waist. His expression remaining the same, his right hand slowly came up and slid beside her head, with his fingers behind her ear and his thumb on her temple. He brought her in with the perfect combination of force and tenderness, kissing her.*

*Those eyes.*

Her hand left her hip and found its way to her right knee, where it made a slow and deliberate U-turn towards her inner thigh. Her wrist was loose and her entire body felt as though it was trapped in slow-motion.

*The kiss started gently and became more passionate. Both her hands left his waist and came up to his smooth, young face. His hands fell down to her waist, and he brought her in tightly so that his hips bumped against hers. She wrapped her thighs around his right leg.*

She slipped her panties aside and allowed her fingers to dance a ballet of ecstasy, tracing slow circles in the rhythms of her fantasy. The gentle wind that blew into the room caused the candle on the nightstand to dance with her.

*Those eyes. Those eyes.*

When she was finished, she lay there, looking at the ceiling and wondering what had come over her.

Later that night, in the bath, she gave a good deal of thought to what exactly was going on in her head. Finally, she decided to play psychologist. At the paper, she was charged with thanklessly covering menial stories in a dull town, and she was constantly frustrated by her inability to get her sister on track. Her relationship with her mother was in shambles. This simple piece of paper was a weapon; one that, if used, would irreparably disrupt the only thing that made sense: her life with Shaun. It felt good to have a secret. She was excited by this power. She felt strong and mysterious. She felt sexual.

Melissa climbed out of the bathtub, dried herself off, and made dinner for one.

The next day, anticipating more drama at the office, she slipped the piece of paper into her jacket pocket. She had no intention of ever calling Roman, and was in fact much more infatuated with the piece of paper than she was with the man himself.

# 11

"Did you see this?"

Melissa was staring absently at a blank computer monitor when Bennett threw the piece of paper onto her desk. She looked at it quizzically.

"Another fire?"

"Yeah, another hospital. No serious injuries this time though. Looks like faulty wiring in the nurses' lounge set it off."

Melissa looked dumbfounded. "This makes no sense."

Bennett nodded. "Great minds think alike."

Melissa turned to her computer and began to type. "Maybe we can look into the companies that wired these buildings. They're all older, slightly run-down. Maybe they all used the same electrician or company." She paused and looked up at him again. "We may have ourselves a nice cage-rattling piece on our hands."

Bennett just looked at her, his face serious. "You're two steps behind me. I ran a check. No real overlap." He took a few steps towards the door, paused for a second, looked to the ground, and then turned back to her. "It's an arsonist."

Melissa stared past him. "Who's your source?"

Bennett raised his voice slightly. "My gut, dammit. What else could this be? It's past obvious that these aren't all coincidences."

Melissa turned to him directly. "Bullshit."

"Bullshit? Do you think your boy toy and his buddies over at the engine will tell you? I'm sure this is one conversation he doesn't want to bring up, especially with you."

Melissa glared for a moment, making sure her emotions didn't get the best of her. Conjuring a kindly tone, she said, "Bennett, I think you really have to drop this conspiracy crap."

"And I think you need to pull your head out of your ass." Bennett was now full-on yelling. "Melissa, the old you would be out at the car right now, running to that hospital, and getting into those prick firefighters' faces about what they're covering up."

His anger dissipated slightly. "You're too subjective on this one. It's too close to home, and you're blind to it."

# 12

As Shaun walked into his house, the first thing he saw was Melissa sitting on his couch with her arms crossed, a scowl very prominently resting on her brow. He jumped. For a moment, he had forgotten that she had a key.

"We need to talk," she said, daggers dripping out of not just her eyes, but her voice as well.

Shaun smiled. "Hello to you, too!"

He took his shoes off and made his way over to the couch, a little too casually, given Melissa's disposition. As he sat, he continued to smile at her, as if he knew what she now suspected. Her anger bubbled over.

"So, when were you going to tell me it was an arsonist?"

The smile quickly vanished from his face. "What?"

"Don't bullshit me. How long have you suspected it was an arsonist?"

Shaun stared through her. "It's good to see you too," he said calmly. "Now maybe you should leave."

He got up and made his way to the front door, his body visibly tense. Melissa shot up from the couch, her hands balled into fists.

"Is it true?"

Shaun paused, his hand resting on the doorknob. He said nothing.

"Why didn't you tell me?" Melissa's voice almost quivered as she said it, but her anger alone kept it steady. She realized that most of her anger stemmed from the fact that she felt foolish for not realizing this herself when Bennett had, rather than the fact that Shaun hadn't told her. Was she angry at Shaun or herself?

Shaun exhaled and turned towards her.

"We came to the conclusion yesterday. Before, it seemed like a possibility, but there was no rhyme or reason to it. Usually, there's..." Shaun trailed off for a moment, trying to find the right word. "Usually there's...a pattern." He leaned against the door, his arms resting on the small of his back, his eyes looking towards the ground. "But this one had none."

Melissa let the anger drop. "Was it the second hospital? Do they think that's where the pattern is?"

Shaun raised his eyes level to her. "Yes and no. They think the second hospital was a way of throwing off the scent. They think no pattern may *be* the pattern."

Melissa was puzzled. "That doesn't really make any sense. You guys didn't even know there was an arsonist."

"But he knew we'd get there. The investigators think he overplayed his hand." Shaun said.

"But still..."

Shaun raised his voice for the first time during the exchange and cut her off. "I don't know, Melissa, I'm not an investigator, I'm just helping them with some information. I'm not a part of this crazy conspiracy you're fabricating in your head."

Melissa glared at him, surprised by his sudden anger. "Why are you yelling at me?"

"You came in here, accusing me of withholding information from you, all aggressive...all..."

"You *were* the one withholding information from me, Shaun. You."

"It's my job, Melissa. Just because you're a reporter, just because you're my girlfriend, doesn't give you some special right. I don't have to..."

He stopped, and looked down at the floor for a moment.

"How's this for sharing information?" he said, "I'd like you to get the fuck out of my house."

# 13

Melissa sat on her couch, eyes slightly glazed, watching television. A glass dangled between her fingers and a half empty bottle of chardonnay sat on the coffee table. The local news was showing live footage of a fire investigation unfolding downtown. Melissa took notice of Shaun in the background, standing amidst the rubble of what had once been a warehouse used by a chain of local convenience stores. The warehouse—like the many businesses that had once peppered the landscape—had been abandoned after the economy crashed back around 2008.

Melissa hadn't spoken with Shaun since their fight a few nights prior, and the regret and anger surrounding their last encounter kept her stubborn. She took another sip of wine. Dan Harris was visibly annoyed on the television set now, and the bottom third of the screen was lit up with bad "fire" special effects and the tagline "Valley Arsonist?"

She ran a story about the arsonist, and now she regretted doing so.

One large final sip and the alcohol was gone. She hiccupped slightly and poured herself another glass. Dammit, she wished he'd just call. Was he furious? Indifferent? This strange limbo was starting to weigh heavily on her, and with each passing day she felt more and more that the relationship may be at its end.

She leaned over to the coffee table and picked up the familiar now-frayed piece of paper; something that she found herself doing more and more, especially after a glass of wine or two had entered her system.

Why could she not get Roman out of her thoughts? In a way, he scared her; his words were abrupt, his soul detached and strangely inhuman. But those eyes, god—they burned into her like nothing had before. Her mind traveled back to that hospital room.

Despite her best efforts, he remained an enigma to her. The nice thing about being a reporter—and the nice thing about him being a survivor of one of those fires—was that she could look up whatever she wanted about him and just say it was for an article. She could justify it as residual research from his being burned in the explosion. The problem was that barely anything turned up. She had gotten ahold of his hospital record from that day, and determined that the mysterious stranger was Roman Carver, 27, and that he had indeed been treated for a mild burn. Further research divulged very little; no arrests, no warnings, no drunk driving. No registered pets, no house title, no jaywalking. He was so clean, he could probably fail to pay his taxes without anyone noticing.

This all just made him that much more mysterious, and by default, attractive to her. She damned him for not only or playing to her weakness, but also for introducing her to that very weakness.

She took another sip of wine. Her head began to swim.

There was only one real way to find anything out. She picked her phone up, and gave Roman a call.

# 14

It was raining.

Actually, it was pouring, and the water hitting the concrete sounded like radio static. The air felt like the hot breath of an invisible life force, overlooking the city and panting in the same rhythm as Melissa's labored heartbeat. She had never been this nervous in her life.

Melissa found herself in her car, windows fogged, outside Roman's house. She checked her watch habitually, and—realizing that she hadn't even seen the time—looked again. 9:51PM.

She wasn't sure how she expected to find this strange man living, but the house was average. A thin-but-tall older single home on a street mostly populated comprised of twins. The neighborhood was nondescript and middle-class. Domestic. For a moment, she thought his house may be slightly crooked, but then determined that it was merely the slant of the street and lawn that created the illusion.

She thought back to the phone call. For the fourth or fifth time, she replayed it in her mind.

*The phone rang three times before Roman picked up. He didn't say a word. After a few seconds of silence, Melissa spoke up.*

*"Hello?"*

*"Hello," Roman said.*

*"This is—my name is Melissa. I don't know if you remember me, but we spoke at the hospital."*

*"I do indeed remember you. How's the injury? Well healed I hope."*

*Melissa was taken aback. After scouring her mind for a moment and trying to recall the injury he may be referring to, she remembered why she had been in the hospital. She said, "I wasn't injured."*

*"And yet you found your way into a hospital. Life's curious, isn't it?"*

*As tended to be the case during conversations with Roman, the conversation took an unexpected direction, laughing in the face of any established social norms. Melissa found herself speechless, guarded, and vaguely insulted. She was about to say something—though she was unsure what, exactly—when he continued.*

*"I'm glad you called me. I was hoping you would. I would have called you, but in your rush to leave, you forgot to give me your phone number."*

Melissa snapped out of the flashback. She shut her eyes, just as she had when Roman said the line she was replaying in her mind. She imagined his soul-piercing eyes, and tried to take in the fact that she'd be seeing them soon. She had altered the encounter at the hospital so dramatically throughout the course of her fantasies during the last few weeks that she now remembered him standing much closer to her than he actually had.

Melissa fell back into the memory of the phone call.

*She found courage and decided to play his game a bit. "Well, I called you. Impress me."*

*She wasn't sure what that even meant.*

*Roman quickly exhaled in such a way that Melissa could tell that he was smiling. He said, "Come over. I don't trust telephones. I find that an inability to share body language can cause context and intention to become misconstrued. 818 Wharf."*

*Melissa hung up the phone instinctually. At first, she thought that she had done so out of fear—what the hell was she doing? What sort of psychopath was this guy? Every sentence was weirder than the last.*

55

*After a moment, however, she realized that she had hung up in such a hurry because she couldn't wait to leave to meet him.*

She opened her eyes. Back in the foggy tomb, surrounded by torrential rain, she decided to make a run for the front door on the count of three. She sighed. One, two, three. She flung open the door, and the sound of the rain multiplied in volume without the buffer caused by her car's doors and windows.

Melissa let out a yelp, and threw her hand to her mouth; standing directly next to her car door was Roman, holding an umbrella. She slowly stood, massively intimidated. Her eyes were wide, her mouth open, her breathing fast. As if pulled in by a tractor beam, she brought herself close to him. He smiled, shut her car door without breaking eye contact, and began walking toward the house.

# 15

Melissa looked at her watch. 1:18AM.

She was sitting on a wonderfully comfortable and well-worn couch, curled with her hands wrapped around her knees, though she wasn't doing so in a defensive way, or because she was cold. For the past few hours, Melissa and Roman conversed. His house was welcoming and well-kept. Prints of obscure jazz musicians adorned the walls, which were mostly tan, save for the occasional stark red accent wall. The floors were bare, expensive-looking wood. The house was old and roomy, and it looks as though a perfectly normal person lived there.

However, this was not the case; with every word that came out of his mouth, Roman proved to be stranger than Melissa had previously thought. She learned a good deal about him, and every piece of information he divulged seemed to add to the mystique that surrounded him.

Roman inquired about Melissa's upbringing and current family life. He was harshly straightforward, and asked questions in a manner that would normally be considered rude: "has anyone very close to you died?" Nonetheless, Melissa found his bluntness refreshing. He seemed genuinely interested in her past and present life, and truly and convincingly listened when she spoke.

She opened up completely to him. She felt as though she didn't have a choice. She felt strangely comfortable, as though she was dreaming or watching a film about someone else's experience that would be erased when she walked away. He offered her a drink and brought back wine. Apparently he didn't drink alcohol, dismissively quipping, "I have too much to think about to have that to deal with. I resent the fact that I have to sleep enough as it is; I don't need something else wasting my time." He apparently kept the wine in the house because "guests expect it and it's less tiresome to keep wine on hand than it is to have a conversation about why I have none." This apparently also explained the jazz prints; buying a few pieces of decor is apparently easier than having a conversation about one's bare walls. She couldn't really find a flaw in his reasoning. She felt as though she wanted to ask, "But don't you like having a nice home?" but found herself feeling foolish for even desiring such petty, earthly things in the presence of someone so enlightened. So honest and comfortable with themselves. He didn't listen to music, but read extensively. While thinking of this, she looked around to find a television, but—as she expected—found none.

As it turned out, Roman made an astounding amount of money simply by leveraging legal loopholes in credit card incentive programs. He would open multiple cards in the names of multiple small businesses that he owned, make specific purchases from partner companies, and earn massive amounts of travel miles or "points." He would then turn around and sell them to third parties at a discounted rate. With his apparently intensive knowledge of the system (and finance as a whole), he managed to procure these miles very easily, and the individuals to whom he sold the miles (which he called "middle brokers") would sell them to a select group of wealthy eastern European businessmen and playboys who travel frequently enough for it to be worthwhile to purchase travel rights in bulk.

She didn't fully understand; it was quite a bit to take in, she was a bit dizzy with drink, and she didn't even know credit card points could be transferred. She dropped it, but considered the fact that the unorthodox nature of this line of work seemed to fit Roman incredibly well.

They talked at length about Melissa's job ("if the news didn't tell people what was important, how would they know?") and life in Washington Valley ("you've got to live and die somewhere, I'd prefer to do it someplace quiet"). His perspective continually fascinated Melissa, who drank in every word as though she were reading a book of famous quotations. When Melissa brought up the recent string of fires, her mysterious host seemed to become incredibly focused. Since Roman had been injured in one such blaze, Melissa cursed herself and thought that she may have breached a sore subject matter. Roman fixed his eyes on the red wall behind Melissa, and said with incredible care,

"The malls—the malls just seem pointless. The drug houses, I suppose a bit of twisted karmic justice. But—the hospitals and retirement homes are..."

He seemed genuinely emotional for the first time since she'd met him. "The hospitals and retirement homes are universally tragic. Pure, misdirected evil."

After some time, the wine, the red walls, the lighting, and the addition of humanity to Roman's piercing eyes began to relax Melissa even more. Staring into the flame of a nearby candle in the otherwise still room, she felt as though she were entering a state between sleep and wakefulness, and excused herself to the bathroom.

"It's the door on the right," Roman said.

Melissa stood up. She became suddenly very aware of the sounds of her body—her heartbeat, her breathing, her swallowing. She began to walk down the hallway, and turned towards a door on the left.

"The *right*," Roman called out in a somewhat brash tone. Melissa snapped back to reality for a brief moment, raised her hand as if to say, "Yes, right, sorry," and proceeded to the bathroom.

She sat down on the closed toilet seat and rubbed her eyes. She truly felt as though she were living someone else's life—driving their decisions as though she were playing some strange game. She laughed.

Well, she thought, if I am at the driver's seat of someone else's life, I might as well make the ride fun.

Roman looked up to find Melissa completely nude, standing at the entrance to the hallway. He didn't seem to react, but slowly took her in and seemed to memorize her, his eyes falling slowly from her head to her toes like a single droplet of water making its way down her body. She shivered and walked toward him.

# 16

Melissa stared at Shaun's house. More specifically, she stared at the lone light that shined from his living room window. It'd been over a week since the blow-up at his house and by now, she genuinely missed him. The guilt of her fling with Roman wasn't helping any either. She told herself it wasn't cheating, as the lack of communication between her and Shaun was obviously his way of saying goodbye, regardless of how childish it was. Every time she had this thought, however, she questioned just how much she believed it and how much she thought it in order to make herself feel less guilty.

Regardless, they were done, but it didn't mean she couldn't have some closure, or to at least something close to it. She just wanted a simple conversation and to lay it all out. Make sure they were on the same page. But then, why was she having such a hard time making her way to the door? "Fuck it", she said, as she hoisted the box of Franzia under her left arm and walked down the path. Her heart beat in rhythm with the noise from the pebbles on the walkway as she made her way toward the front door.

A slow, deliberate movement interrupted the light in the window as Shaun got up from his couch and turned to look out at her. She saw his shadowed head shake in the lamplight before he disappeared into the other room. Melissa put her head down, partly due to a vague sense of guilt and partly due to a renewed determination, and made her way forward. The butterflies had started to fly about in her stomach. The door opened slightly as she approached. Suddenly, there he was.

"I brought you a box of wine", she said, a sheepish smile on her face as she dangled the box's carry-string between her fore and middle fingers.

"Very classy", he said, his icy gaze throwing her off-balance. Melissa fought back a wave of emotions as her eyes met his. She knew this was a bad idea.

Shaun sighed and opened the door wider. "You should come in…" he said, trailing off slightly. "But only if you plan to share."

# 17

They sat across from each other in complete silence. Light from the muted TV flickered as they both avoided eye contact. Melissa played with the coffee mug in her hands, swirling the wine around and seeing how close she could get it to the rim. She hadn't really thought through what she'd say when she finally got in the door; in truth, until she saw Shaun's face, the idea of actually conversing with him seemed unlikely. She raised her head to speak, but Shaun beat her to the punch.

"It was real shitty what you did, you know. Publishing a story based on what I thought was a private conversation?" He shifted in his seat before he continued. "Half of the house thinks I'm a narc now, and that's never good for business."

Melissa hung her head back down and began to fight back some tears. She knew it then and she knew it now, but hearing him say it out loud was another thing entirely. "What do you want to do, then?" she asked, raising her head to meet his eyes.

Shaun just shrugged his shoulders. "Apologize? I'm not sure. I still don't know why I even let you in here."

Melissa nodded. "I'm sorry."

Shaun just snickered and shook her head. It made her feel small and angry, even though she knew it was a half-assed apology. She placed the mug of wine on his coffee table and started to rise. Maybe this...thing that was starting with Roman was worth seeing out further. Obviously, this wasn't going to work.

"Wait."

Shaun was also now standing and looked at her with puppy-dog eyes. For the first time, she really got the sense of how hurt he truly was.

"I don't mean to be shitty", he said, taking a step towards her. "I'm angry. I'm sad. I'm just...emotions right now. I'm raw."

He now stood in front of her, his hand under her chin as Melissa stared down at the ground. God, he did something to her, even when she'd finally convinced herself to move on. These damn men were nothing but trouble for her. She looked up and met Shaun's eyes.

"You're worth working through this. You're not...typical. I want to see where this goes."

His lips found hers. Melissa returned the kiss.

# 18

Shaun gently took Melissa's hand with his and led her to his bedroom, his other hand clumsily unbuttoning his plaid shirt. A slight tremble shooting through his fingers. The nervous vibrations made the hairs on her arm stand on end.

She tried to stay in the moment, but her mind wandered to the other night.

*A Bare-chested Roman pushed open the door, his blue eyes never breaking contact with Melissa's as he led her into his room. His hands hungrily unbuttoned her blouse, her own hand brushing against his scarred forearm.*

Shaun smiled and kissed Melissa on the lips as he gently pulled her sweater over her head and tossed it to the side of his bed.

*Roman tossed Melissa's bra to the floor and took in her bare, perky breasts. In one swift motion, he lifted her in the air, her legs wrapping around his back as he buried his face into her chest, his tongue hungrily flicking against her nipple.*

Melissa unbuckled Shaun's belt and smiled up at him playfully as she unzipped his jeans and slid her hands under his boxers, gently squeezing his chiseled ass in her hands as she slipped his jeans off. The moment was tender and familiar.

*Melissa gasped as Roman pulled off her capris in one violent motion. She breathed heavily as she looked up at him. He stood naked in front of her, a smirk on his face as he took his already-hard penis in both hands. Melissa stared at it. The moment was tense and exhilarating.*

Shaun gently placed Melissa down on the bed. Her head nestled in the firm pillows as she smiled up at Shaun. He leaned over her and began to lightly kiss the right side of her neck, his fingertips caressing her back, dancing at the cleft of her ass cheeks. She ran her own hands through his light, soft hair.

*Melissa brought her eyes back up to Roman's. She crawled across the bed to him like an animal, her eyes never leaving his. She pushed his hand away and took his penis in her own hand. It was warm and smooth. She slowly began to stroke it, speeding up and feeling it grow ever more rigid.*

Shaun pulled Melissa in close and their lips interlocked. He momentarily broke away, smiling from ear to ear as he took her body in from bottom to top. Melissa returned the smile, pulling her skirt down slowly and savoring the anticipation.

*Roman lifted Melissa up suddenly and the two began to kiss. Melissa pulled away about an inch, biting and holding his lip as she did so, a dead-serious look in her eyes. Roman let out a small noise and flipped Melissa over, pulling her panties off as he did so in one smooth motion.*

Melissa let out a low moan as she guided Shaun into her. His hands rested on her waist as he followed her motions. She increased her speed and the two stayed in perfect sync. His fingers pressed slightly into her hips as the pace quickened. Suddenly, his back stiffened and he grabbed her close, letting out a long moan as her fingers gently made their way down his back.

*Melissa let out a deep moan as Roman took her from behind. He entered her in a way that was at the same time sudden and comfortable. He pulled her in close, her ass slapping against his hips as the two made love in an almost panicked rhythm. Melissa felt him deep inside her, a heat and pressure rising in her hips, her thighs, her chest. She came twice, only seconds apart—something that she had never before experienced. Her eyes were wide, her mouth open. She could make no noise. She gave herself completely to this man, this moment. With a sudden and animalistic cry, Roman collapsed onto her, breathing rapidly directly into the back of her neck. She reached back and caressed his leg.*

Melissa lay on Shaun's chest, listening to him breathe. He stared up at the ceiling, a smile on his face as his breath found its normal pace. Melissa stared off into space, replaying the very different sex that had transpired the night before.

*Melissa and Roman lay naked on the bed, both madly out of breath and covered in sweat, the bed sheets disrupted and pillows strewn across the room. Roman rested on his elbows, smiling in a way that she hadn't yet seen from him. Melissa chuckled and sighed, happily. She hadn't felt this satisfied in a very long time.*

Shaun ran his left hand through her hair, his right hand resting on her thigh. He squeezed it gently, turning his gaze down at her, his smile playful. "So I guess this means that we're speaking again?"

Melissa turned onto her side, running her finger down the side of his leg. "If that's what you want."

Shaun nodded. "Let's take it day by day."

*Roman rose from the bed, stretching his naked frame in the moonlight that snuck into the room from the window. The bluish glow cast shadows between his abs and in the valleys of his chest, making him look like a sculpture. He turned to her. "I enjoyed that conversation." He picked his shirt off of the ground and began to wipe the sweat from his brow.*

*Melissa propped herself up, resting on the palms of each hand.*

*"Well, we should talk more often then."*

*Roman looked down at her, dropped the shirt, and began walking toward her again. She looked down between his legs, where she saw him growing again.*

*"You know," he said with a smile, "I thought of something else to say..."*

# 19

"Yeah. I can. Uh-huh. No, Dan already told me."

Shaun was pacing back and forth just inside the front door. He was wearing gray Adidas running shorts and a sleeveless black UnderArmor shirt.

"Should I meet you at the station?"

The phone had already been ringing when Shaun got home from his run, and he picked it up on what was probably the last possible second. Shaun was still catching his breath, and Melissa could immediately tell from his tone that the subject matter was important. She watched him intently throughout the conversation, trying to figure out what exactly was afoot.

"Will do. Just let me know if you need me to bring anything."

The overhead light made the sweat on his skin shine, and when he stopped to end the call, his neck and collarbone seemed as though they were lit up from inside. He sat the phone down in the little tray that holds their keys. He sat down on the floor, with his back leaning against the couch. This was a strange habit of his; after working out, Shaun didn't want to get sweat on the furniture, so instead of heading right to the shower, he'd sit on the floor.

Melissa didn't inquire, instead waiting for Shaun to say something; however, she didn't stop watching him. He seemed tense. When he realized that she was still watching him, he said, "That was the cops. They want me to help with the investigation."

Melissa knew exactly which investigation Shaun was referring to—it was everywhere, in the very heartbeat of the town. The Washington Valley Firebug had struck four times in as many weeks: Decatur Medical Center, Northeastern Hospital, and twice at the WV Mall.

"What? Why you?"

"Well, I'm the one who filed the final reports for the last four and was IC for the last two. I guess they just needed somebody who had been there."

IC meant "incident commander." The boss man. *El jefe.*

"My squad was also first responder on the last one."

Melissa gave Shaun a crooked look that implied that he was being modest and that she was seeing through it. Their eyes met and he conceded. "Dan suggested they talk to me."

Melissa stood up and walked over to him. He reached for her hand, and she was surprised to find that her immediate reaction was to pull it away. She managed not to show this, and offered it to him without missing a beat. Inside, however, she felt ashamed. Things like that had been happening since they decided to continue their relationship, but she couldn't quite understand why. She sat down next to him on the floor.

She played with his fingers, trying to overcompensate for the cold reaction that her instincts had provided her. "Well, that's good, you know, with you being worried about—job security and whatnot. Means that you're valued. Valuable."

Shaun laughed quietly.

"What?" Melissa asked.

"Nothing, it's just—yeah, you're right."

Shaun sensed Melissa's confusion and continued, "It's just, I should be glad about that, but then, I don't know, should I really be glad?" He looked over to find Melissa's face still exhibiting confusion. He shut his eyes, leaned his head back, and said, "It's like being a coroner. And being glad that you have job security because a ton of people are dropping dead. Good for you, bad for—society."

They both laughed, the first time they had done so in almost a month. It felt natural and warm. They both seemed to sit there for a moment and bask in it. Eventually, Melissa asked what Shaun would be doing in regards to the investigation. "I don't know," Shaun replied, "detective work? Kind of exciting." He lowered his voice and cocked his eyebrow at Melissa. "I'm on the pyro case."

"Well, that makes two of us," Melissa said, slapping Shaun's knee and standing. "The last story got a lot of traction, and I start my next one tomorrow."

# 20

Melissa had to double check the letter one more time, just to make sure that the message was, in fact, not a figment of her imagination. She found it odd that she had received an envelope addressed to her in the first place—most of her hate mail had migrated over to email years ago—and found it slightly scary that it had no return address in the upper left corner. After briefly contemplating the possibility of it being contaminated with anthrax, she quickly shook the thought from her head and opened the envelope by running a nail file along the top. A carefully folded piece of yellow legal paper fell into her hand, containing the following message:

*To Whom It May Concern,*

*Your coverage paints an interesting picture, but you got the colors wrong. Make my acquaintance at the Crossing Diner Thursday 8PM.*

*No cops. No bullshit. One chance.*

*- Saint Agatha*

Melissa's heart raced. Her second article had been the headline story two days prior, this time with the full cooperation of Shaun and the fire department. The fires were becoming more frequent, leading the authorities to open up some, if only to calm a skittish populace down for just a few days.

And now, in front of her, sat a mystery.

Saint Agatha? She thought about the strange salutation for a moment before looking the handle up on the Internet. A few moments of research revealed that Saint Agatha was the Catholic patron saint of fire.

Melissa smiled. Was this a dare? A taunt? Like a movie, the firebug seemed to be attempting to engage her in a game of cat and mouse. A part of her thought it had to be an elaborate hoax, something an asshole frat kid from State had put together to high-five his brothers about in between games of beer pong. Maybe when she showed up, they'd spray her down with Natty Ice and say something witty.

Deep down, though, she knew it wasn't the case; this was the real McCoy. A pang of terror crept from her neck and ran down her spine. She shivered. She instinctively reached for her phone, but paused. This may be the only chance anyone would have to speak with this person. And hopefully stop him. Maybe she could wear a wire? Or be monitored from afar? She pulled her hand back and rested it on her leg, her fingers dancing nervously on her knee caps. No. She'd do it alone. *No cops. No bullshit. One chance.*

# 21

On her way back to her apartment, Melissa devised a plan to ensure that there'd be a trail to follow, should something happen to her. She sent a text to Terry, telling her she was going to the diner to catch up with an old friend and that she'd give her a call later. She also circled the date and time in her planner, address included, and left it on the side table by her bed. Between that and Terry, she figured the authorities could piece things together, should she be kidnapped...or worse. She knew it was slightly ridiculous, but understood the power of a paper trail and figured a little insurance wouldn't hurt...

She took a quick shower and changed into a red summer dress. She hoped this would allow her to be remembered by someone, but a small part of her also wanted to exhibit confidence. Red meant power, and she hoped it gave the impression that she wasn't scared, even if her arm hair was still standing on end while initially reading the letter. She picked out a pair of silver sandals and, with a deep breath, made her way to her car.

The ride over to the diner seemed to take forever. She put on some talk radio, hoping that the riled-up, slightly racist host would anger her so much that she'd become distracted, at least for a few seconds here and there. Instead, her plan had the opposite effect; the host's daily dose of anger was directed at the arsonist, bringing his usual fire and brimstone rhetoric to highlight points that she couldn't help but agree with, much to her dismay.

Worse, it brought the reality of this meeting back down to earth and Melissa began to realize just how idiotic this idea really was. She could be killed, and that was a very real thing. Unfortunately, this realization came as she pulled into the diner's parking lot. Melissa took a moment to compose herself and turned the car off. It was time.

The diner was fairly empty. An old couple sat in the corner. A few college kids sat somewhere near the center, loudly carousing with one another, and leaving Melissa wondering if they, in fact, were the collective "man behind the curtain" as she half-suspected earlier. Aside from them, there wasn't much. A scattering of middle-aged couples silently eating and staring at their plates. No one sitting by themselves, however. Melissa wondered what he would even look like. Was it even a "he?" Maybe it was one of the waitresses here. A young girl with an off-bronze name badge that read "Rachel" interrupted Melissa's thoughts and led her to her table. She couldn't be more than sixteen, Melissa thought. No way she's an arsonist mastermind. Melissa tried to remember whether or not she had ever heard of a female arsonist; she attempted to review ten years of journalism experience in a few seconds, and came to the realization that the perpetrator was indeed most likely a male, white, and between the ages of twenty and fifty. Fire has a type.

She ordered a cup of coffee in hopes it would settle her nerves, or at least to give the illusion that it was the cause of her nervous shaking. Rachel brought it out and Melissa added two packs of sugar and a dash of half & half. Then, she began the waiting process.

Two hours passed and the man behind the curtain hadn't showed. An empty pie plate sat next to her thrice-filled coffee cup. Melissa tapped on the

71

counter, her irritation intensified by the exorbitant amount of caffeine now coursing through her veins. She felt stupid and silly for thinking that this was anything more than a prank. With a sigh, Melissa grabbed the check that Rachel had left for her as her shift ended and paid for her meal at the register.

Melissa made her way to the car and pulled out her keys. Her hands shook with anger now as she fumbled to unlock her car door. Behind the anger, a small sense of relief boiled to the surface, followed by another, more sinister thought. Was he watching her? Was this all a test? Melissa closed the door behind her and quickly hit the lock. Even if these thoughts were mere flights of fancy, she'd still keep a close eye on her rear-view mirror. Her heart quickened, even though she wasn't sure whether it was due to legitimate fear or the excitement of finding herself in the middle of this strange game.

# 22

As Melissa's car pulled up to a red light, she noticed that her phone was vibrating in the passenger seat beside her. She had switched it to silent so that it wouldn't ring while she sat at the diner; she didn't want to draw any unnecessary attention. Not knowing how many times it had rung, she sprang for it eagerly, in case it was the arsonist. Unable to hide her urgency, she yelled into the phone: "Hello!"

"What's with the bizarro text?"

Terry. After realizing that the arsonist probably wouldn't have her cell number, she felt a bit silly. "What?"

"The text. Was that meant for me?"

Melissa rubbed her eyes. The light turned green. "Yeah, that was meant for you," she said, and, predicting further inquiry, followed up with a white lie. "I was going to send you more details, but then I realized that you didn't know the person. Thought you did."

After a moment of silence, Terry asked, "who was it?" Although this was the obvious follow-up question, it took Terry off-guard. For a second, she contemplated hanging up, regaining her composure, and then calling back, saying the call dropped. Instead, she just said, "Jen Sullivan. From camp." She proceeded to tactfully change the subject, luring Terry into a predictable diatribe about their mother. While Terry was ranting, Melissa calmed her breathing and regained control.

When she pulled up to her house, it started to rain lightly. She felt something welling up inside her. Something foreign and frightening. She put Terry on speakerphone, sat the phone on the car's dashboard, and silently cried into her hands. When she closed her eyes, she saw fire. Walls of scorching, wild flames engulfing a shapeless structure in a black void. A tremendous, dull roar like a thousand lions punctuated by sharp staccato crackling. She faded away from her body and immersed herself in the scene. She imagined herself naked, covered in sweat, facing the blaze. Her breath quickened. She looked down, and could see the reflection of the orange blaze reflected off her skin. Roman walked out of the flames and approached her. His shape was dark, as the flames were behind him, but she could tell it was him. She imagined reaching out with her hand. He took it. The heat was unbearable but completely alive and wonderful. He kissed her neck and came around behind her. She shut her eyes and tilted her head back as his hand traced her jaw line, her neck, her shoulder. Almost impossibly gently, the tips of three fingers brushed her right nipple, bringing it instantly to life. A beam of heat shuddered through her body as his hand slid slowly down her stomach and held her inner thigh. She gently pressed her legs together to keep him there. She wanted to stay in this moment as long as she could. She turned to him, seeing the fire reflect in the sweat of his muscular stomach and chest, off his angular, dramatic shoulders. She, Roman, and the fire seemed to merge into one entity as she gently, slowly faded back to reality.

Terry was wrapping up, and Melissa was surprised to hear that she wasn't talking about herself.

"...haven't sounded right the last few times we talked. I just worry about you. You're the one who has it together, so you have to keep it together." Terry laughed. Melissa, sensing that she should be laughing, laughed too, wiping tears from her eyes.

"I'd do anything for you, sis," said Terry. "Anything."

Melissa sniffled and said, "The way things have been going lately, I just might have to hold you to that."

# 23

Termini Mall. Holland Plaza. Maple Glen retirement community (again). The Victoria Mall. Decatur Medical Center (again).

The fires continued for another month, seeming to gain velocity with each passing week. People lost track of the targets and the order of the attacks. The city was aghast and in a state of virtual lockdown. Security heightened. Additional police were brought in from Haddon and Longhurst. It all seemed like a strange dream.

Until Dozzy Dosewicz died.

Gerald "Dozzy" Dosewicz was a skinny, freckled 18-year old kid with a goofy, toothy smile that personified the very ideal of the American teenager. He graduated from WV High, where he ran cross country and acted in last year's production of *Annie Get Your Gun*. He played in a band with some friends every Sunday afternoon in his parents' garage. He went fishing, dated Mara Osburn, and was working for a year before studying education at State.

He died after rushing into the fire at Decatur, thinking his mother, Janet—a registered nurse—was still inside. Not three seconds after he broke the fireman's grip and disappeared into the wall of smoke, the entire building collapsed on itself, the sound of crashing lumber and steel dulled by the deafening rumble of flames. Despite the obvious implication of the collapse, everyone just stared at the remains of the building; there was no catharsis, no finality. The air was thick with collective disbelief. The flattening building let out a massive plume of pitch-black smoke, as though it were the boy's soul and the town's heart escaping into the ether. The crowd stared, mouths agape, until Janet broke the silence and unspoken hope with a scream that would forever haunt everyone in attendance.

Washington Valley abruptly stopped dreaming and woke up with a start. Pure, undignified sadness overtook the entire town, which was quickly overrun by makeshift posters, flower arrangements, and knowing nods and head-shakes. This sadness, however, would only last a few days, as it was quickly nudged out of the way by an unabashed and sharply-directed anger. Sentiment towards the Washington Valley Firebug became vulgar and violent, and began to manifest itself in resentment towards the authorities, who seemed clueless, ill-prepared, and unable to protect the taxpayers.

# 24

616 Wesley Street. 2100 Martin Luther King Blvd. 12924 North Tioga Street.

Melissa was sitting on her couch at 12:19AM on a Monday morning. The room was dark, except for the light from a small lamp on the table next to her. It cast a shadowy caramel circle on the carpet before her. Wearing only panties and a t-shirt, Melissa sat completely forward, with her feet on the floor and her chest leaning against her knees. She looked down at the sea of papers and photographs that lay before her.

At least half of this mess began on her computer, but Melissa had printed them out. She worked better with physical, tangible artifacts that she can easily move and rearrange. She was visual, tactile.

She stared at the piles before her, and tried to process everything that she had come to realize over the past hour.

616 Wesley Street. 2100 Martin Luther King Blvd. 12924 North Tioga Street. Known drug houses, burned to the ground last year. There were no casualties, minimal police and fire activity, and but a blurb in the paper.

Three months later, the hospitals and malls started going up. They got a lot of attention, but at the same time, 600 14th Street and 412 Barnaby went up. Drug houses, some deaths.

The hospitals and malls continued, and then the whole block at 18th and McGonicle went up. Manny Goza and Gabriel Hernandez died, and others—including Roman—were hurt.

At this point, the hospital and mall fires began to occur at an alarming and quickening pace, while the drug den fires abruptly ceased.

Melissa cursed her notes; she was so unaccustomed to covering stories of real importance that she had become sloppy and complacent. Her handwriting was garbage, and she often made notes that meant as little to her as they would to a stranger (such as a circle with the words "twice/never???" written within it).

However, three days ago, Shaun had brought home a manila envelope containing notes from the police investigation. Without even a second to consider the ethical implications of doing so, Melissa emptied the envelope and photocopied everything. Now, these copies lay before her, strewn about in haphazard piles among other papers.

Patterns began to emerge. The two different types of fires (hospital/mall and drug den) exhibited drastically different attributes.

The hospital and mall incidents began in low-activity rooms and areas; clearly, the fires involved some meticulous planning and infiltration. They typically began in back rooms, and spread slowly, only being noticed when they were already significant. She recently found out that the fire alarms, smoke detectors, and sprinkler systems had all been disabled in each of these cases.

In stark contrast, the drug den fires seemed to be more like explosions; sudden, violent, simplistic. Living rooms and foyers, mostly, as though the bombs were thrown through a front window.

The patterns themselves carried no reason, no sense, no explanation. Melissa hugged her legs and stared, awaiting a revelation that she thought would never come.

Suddenly, a question occurred to her as though it fell from the ceiling onto the paper mound before her—a question which seemed so incredibly obvious now that she felt foolish for not having asked it the second Roman gave her his address over the phone: Why was Roman in one of the worst neighborhoods in Washington Valley during the fire that burned him when he lives all the way up on the north side? Both Mike Gullio and Shaun had said that Roman was collateral damage—an unknowing passer-by who was "walking home," but that no longer made any sense. Why was he at or near a drug house?

She thought back to Roman's face when she brought the fires up at his house. *"The drug houses, I suppose a bit of twisted karmic justice."*

# 25

Melissa's index and middle fingers danced upon the scar that ran up Roman's forearm, tracing out the geography where newer flesh had replaced old as he slept soundly next to her. She'd always assumed this scar was new, received on that day they'd met at the hospital, but the ridges and colors were too dull; they should still have been pink. No, this was a scar that had long ago become familiar.

It was almost funny to Melissa that she couldn't have pieced it together earlier. Was she caught up in the obvious heat of the moment, and so distracted by his odd behavior and mannerisms that she had never noticed the age of the wound so prominent on his arm? She stopped herself.

*Not yet. You don't know for sure.*

She carefully turned onto her side, adjusting herself so she could take in Roman's naked torso. Deep, quiet breaths expanded and contracted his chest, the street lights' dim rays through the open window highlighted the small, varied burn scars that pock-marked his upper chest. Had he gotten them at the same time as his arm? She wasn't sure she'd get a chance to ask, but the question was worth asking, even if it wasn't said out loud.

Melissa leaned over and kissed his clavicle. He stirred momentarily, but continued to sleep. She shifted her weight onto her left arm and took him. Regardless of the outcome of what she planned to do, she knew the likelihood of Roman speaking to her again was slim-to-none. She traced her finger down his chest, stopping when she reached the rim of his boxer-briefs. A sad smile crossed her face. With a delicate sigh, she quietly made her way out of the bed.

A cold breeze blew through the window, giving Melissa shivers as she quickly pulled one of Roman's simple hooded sweatshirts over her naked chest. She picked up her pajama bottoms that had carelessly been thrown into the dark room's abyss earlier when she and Roman—she stopped the thought. She didn't want to make this harder than it had to be. She stepped into the pant legs one by one and tied the flannel drawstring tight, if only because it gave her one more second in a room she may never set foot in again. She tiptoed across the floor and reached the door, pausing to take him in one last time. She quietly nodded to herself and cautiously closed the door behind her.

Once she was in the hall, Melissa took a deep breath and gazed over to the door on the left, the one he seemed determined for her not to open when she attempted to find the bathroom during their first night together. She stepped quietly toward the doorway, each creak of the wood heightening her senses and seeming as loud as a baseball breaking through a plate glass window. When she reached the door, she carefully jiggled the brass handle, secretly hoping that it was locked, even as the hinges moaned and it slowly opened. A darkness greeted her, and the top four stairs were the only things made visible by the hall light behind her. She reached her right hand into the dark, carefully running her fingers across the wall until she felt the light switch jutting out. With a flick of her index finger, the steps erupted into a sea of light. She made her way down.

On the last step, Melissa paused, with tears already beginning to run down her cheek. She knew it before she reached the landing, but now her eyes now confirmed it. Dirty rags lay in a pile in the corner of the room, next to a washing machine that felt out of place, its newness and bleach white exterior clashing with the mildewed brick walls and concrete floor. To the machine's right side sat canisters of gasoline and paint thinner, and a ball of cans with a coil of copper tubing spiraling around it, like a snake strangling its prey. She slowly approached it, and an acrid smell began to overpower her as she did. Matches, lighters, and unfamiliar (yet comically ominous) devices lined the shelf above a rust-stained sink. A heavy-duty flashlight sat alongside them, and she found herself reaching for it; there were still more corners she needed to explore.

"There are answers to those questions that are banging around in your pretty cranium."

A chill ran up Melissa's spine and clutched her. She slowly turned around, her eyes wide.

Roman's silhouette was visible as he leaned against the doorway at the top of the stairs, his left leg tucked behind his right as if he was James Dean. Melissa wished she could make out his facial expression to gauge what he felt, or to at least determine the level of danger that she now faced. Her left hand gripped tightly around the body of the flashlight as she readied herself for a confrontation.

Roman slowly made his way down the stairs, his head arched down, as if he was a little boy who just disappointed his mother. Each step was deliberate and paced, almost as if he was buying himself time to come up with a better excuse than the truth. When he reached the final step, he looked at her and shrugged.

The glass of the flashlight's bulb shattered as it connected with his left temple. Melissa kneed him in the groin as he looked at her with shock, knocking him off the final step and onto the cold concrete floor.

Melissa bounded up the steps two at a time, expecting Roman's hand to grab at her ankle and pull her down into the hell that was his evil lair, though the hand never came. As she slammed the door to the basement—if for no other reason than to buy her another moment—she glanced down and saw Roman simply sitting and staring up after her. The door closed, and she was off.

She burst through the front door. In her pocket, she located her car keys, which she had carefully placed with her phone before exploring. Her hand shook terribly as she tried to match the key to the lock. The metal screeched against the car door before finally reaching its mark. She pulled the door closed, slammed her hand down on the lock, and started the car. She glanced back at the house as she shifted into reverse, expecting Roman to come racing out like a villain in a slasher flick. Instead, the door just sat open, moths stupidly flying into the porch light and ricocheting off the bulb's protective glass as they sought the flame.

Melissa pulled her phone out and began to call the police, but stopped. She pulled up her favorites, and called her sister.

"Terry," she said, the name coming out as a sob instead of a word. "I need to talk."

# 26

The headlines, both nationally and locally, prominently featured Roman's face, his left eye black and his lower lip telling the story of a recent confrontation. Each news outlet had given him their own callous and tawdry nickname—the Angel of Death, the Valley Phantom, Nero—to accompany his mug shot. His basement was lit by the news team to look like a den of vice; the rag-filled corner was framed and suggested to look like a bed, where possible unknown victims may have been kept for some other secret purpose left to the imagination. The cans of gasoline were stacked and angled in a way such that every photo would have a haunting, iconic feel. All of these images painted a very clear picture, regardless of the outcome of the impending trial: Roman Carver was guilty.

A flaming effigy had been placed on the pavement outside his house the following day, constructed mostly out of paper-mache newsprint pertaining to the case. The figure was held together by a rusted pipe that had been hammered into a lone spot of dirt peering shyly through the concrete sidewalk. The neighbors walked around wide-eyed and eager as the police combed through the exterior of the house, checking for any traps that may have been set within a hundred yard radius. Neighbors crawled out of the woodwork, painting a portrait of Roman as a detached and antisocial being. If only—they would say, forcing back the tears—they could have done something or said something sooner. Maybe none of this would have happened.

As the second day came to a close, a clearer picture began to form showing how Roman was able to hide himself and his crimes—or, at least, the media began to paint such a picture regardless of the facts. He had a collection of old red plastic gas canisters, purchased over multiple years; their faded colors—depleted from the sun's rays shining in through a small basement window—formed a timeline, detailing of each can's age and level of usage. An unsteady wooden shelving unit held all types of accelerants, from typical lighter fluid to pure alcohol, and even some chemicals in clear plastic bottles that the forensics team had to send away for testing.

The motives, however, still seemed odd. Why burn both a mall and a dilapidated old drug den? With the help of firefighter Shaun Duchane, the Washington Valley police department was able to draw up a conclusion, though its ground shook when stood upon: The motive was a lack of motive.

The belief, according to a quick analysis of Roman's antisocial behavior, was that the fire setting was a sexual compulsion. The nature of the buildings did not matter, as long as Roman was able to, essentially, "get off." They hypothesized that the illusion of randomness distracted police from finding a pattern, allowing Roman a greater swath to spread his flame. It was by dumb luck that an anonymous source, believed to be a possible victim, called in the tip, although his or her whereabouts are not currently known. Regardless, a sense of calm was falling over the city once again.

Though the picture's paint was still wet, the image was undeniable. Washington Valley had caught their arsonist.

# 27

Shaun's eyes rolled back in his head, and he exhaled as though he'd been holding his breath for minutes. Melissa came out of the daze that she had been in, and suddenly found herself feeling very exposed. With Shaun still pulsing inside her, she remained atop him, and covered herself with her arms as though she felt ashamed to be nude.

"Holy shit," Shaun said between breaths. He swallowed loudly, and reached up with his right hand to caress Melissa's forearm. When she didn't react, he understood. "It's okay, it's okay," he cooed to her. Melissa slipped off of Shaun's heaving frame and walked into the bathroom. There, she closed the door, braced herself on the sink, and looked up. When she met her own eyes, she laughed briefly; the sound surprised her. She was scared and confused. The light seemed obnoxiously bright, and, fixing her gaze upon her elbows, she realized that she was trembling. She heard Shaun begin to rustle about in the bedroom.

Normally the more romantic and docile of the two, Melissa had just given Shaun an experience that he would literally never forget. They had begun to make love, and Shaun had situated her into their normal missionary position. Her legs spread apart before him, with her feet flat on the bed and her knees wide, centering his muscular torso in between them. She was still wearing a tee shirt, and Shaun lifted it to kiss her breasts. Melissa looked to her left and attempted to relax, but for some reason, she felt distant and distracted. She stared at an old wooden desk chair next to the bed. It faced her, and upon it sat two books that she was currently reading. She fixated on the text of their spines and imagined that it was not her body that gently swayed with each thrust; rather, she imagined that she was still and the room around them was moving. Her left hand slid up his back and shoulder, coming to rest on the back of his head.

It was then that she imagined Roman in the chair. He was dressed as he had been when she was at his home. She smirked as she imagined him smiling at her.

"Is this what you want?" he asked.

Still smiling, she shook her head from side to side.

"This is your paradigm," Roman said. "This is your life at this very moment. Do what you want with it."

She pressed Shaun's face harder into her breast. He stopped for a moment, taken aback, and then continued gently kissing her.

Roman smiled. Melissa stopped smiling. Her feet left the bed and wrapped around Shaun's lower back. She reached down and gripped his hard behind with both hands, and began to pull him deeper into her with each thrust, encouraging him to become more aggressive. She then began to push him each time he exited her, so as to pull further out and make his strokes longer and deeper; she urged him with her every motion to take advantage of every inch he had and to give to her completely.

Shaun barely responded. Instantly, Melissa had gone from tame to aggressive, completely skipping over any transition in between. She gritted her teeth in anger, slammed her palms into the bed, and rolled Shaun over.

Roman very calmly said, "Very nice."

She mounted him, put her hands on his chest, and began to ride him with a feverish anger. The bed began to make noises that their tame lovemaking had never before exposed. She dug her nails into the skin above his clavicle and brought him deeper and deeper with each bounce. Shocked, Shaun looked up at her with confusion, his face contorted as though his feelings had been hurt. He then shut his eyes as though he were on a roller coaster.

Melissa looked at the chair. Roman nodded and said, "It's not me, but it will do."

"Shut the fuck up," Melissa said aloud. Shaun's eyes darted open. He followed her eyes to the chair, confirmed that it was empty, and looked back at her. He tried to ask, "What?" but all that came out was air as Melissa bore down on him with all her weight. His eyes filled with what seemed like fear.

Very suddenly, Shaun came. She could feel him tighten and pulse within her, and could feel him involuntarily driving himself deeper into her. Melissa paid him no mind, only acknowledging it by letting out an audible breath, and continued to focus on the task at hand. Her breathing became louder. She began to feel very light, as though she was fading away, and suddenly stopped moving up and down. She switched to a clockwise motion—a circular, grinding rhythm, keeping Shaun deep inside her. She leaned forward and pressed her face into the pillow next to his head. She took her hand off his muscular chest and covered his mouth as though to silence him, and used his body like a toy, grinding in a fast, consistent circle until she came, shuddering and holding her breath silently, and pressing forcefully into his face with her hand. She seemed to explode into a ball of heat, and she lost all sense that she had a body at all. She felt like pure energy, alive, uninhibited, and in control. She took Roman's imagined advice did what she wanted with life at that very moment. She just didn't know that this was what she wanted. Or needed.

86

"Bravo," said the man in the chair, silently pantomiming applause.

Melissa was gone, and when she saw the face Shaun was making when she came to, she knew that he had not lived some fantasy, but had instead felt violated. She knew too that Shaun would never be able to give her what she now needed. He would never catch up. He would never find in himself the comfort to simply take what he wanted as she had. She removed her hand from his mouth and saw that his skin was white from the pressure she had placed upon it. She could still feel his heartbeat inside her and, becoming suddenly aware of this, she rose from the bed and walked into the bathroom without looking him in the eye.

# 28

Melissa's phone rang, causing her to jump out of her seat. It had been sitting on a coffee table atop some loose change, so its vibration was accompanied by a metallic crunch that rudely punctuated the unearthly silence of the room.

Despite the fact that she was alone, Melissa felt embarrassed about her reaction and angrily snatched the phone up. The caller came up as "unknown," which usually implied a telemarketer or her wireless carrier. Given the bizarreness of the events of the past few days, she picked it up.

"This Melissa?" asked the voice on the other end.

Her mind asked, "Who is this," but her mouth said, to her surprise, "yes."

There was a moment of silence. The man on the other end said, "We met. At the hospital. My name is Luis. I was the dude who walked in when you and R were talking."

Melissa remembered, but said nothing, trying to quickly piece together what this call could possibly be about. She felt as though all the blood had rushed out of her body.

After she said nothing for a moment, the man continued, "I picked him up from the hospital."

"I remember."

"I have to tell you some things. About R. And the fires." Luis had a very slight Hispanic accent and his voice was soothing, kind, and masculine. Paternal. He sounded trustworthy and real.

Melissa nodded without it ever registering that the man on the other end of the phone could not see her.

"Our boy didn't set all those fires. He wanted me to tell you. He doesn't care what the rest of the world thinks, just you. Well, you and a few of us who get it, but we already know, so..."

Melissa sat down on a book, but didn't bother to move it from the chair.

"He didn't set the hospital fires, or the mall or the old people's home, or none of that," he continued. "He's going to take the fall, let it all get wrapped up together, because he's going away anyway, it doesn't matter. But R just did those downtown houses. He only hit up the people who were destroying the town, selling that shit to kids.

Melissa began to tear up. Her lip quivering, her next exhaled breath carried with it a small and pathetic sound. She quickly threw a cupped hand over it and stared straight ahead.

"It's hard to explain," Luis said. "R is a good man. A noble man. He just wanted you to know he wasn't trying to hurt innocent people."

More silence.

Melissa finally took her hand away from her mouth. Her breathing became more rapid and she felt angry and hurt. She couldn't explain it.

"Why?" she asked.

Another few moments of silence passed before Luis replied.

"R and his family grew up down here, before it got bad. When the gangs started running shit, all the old families moved out, started moving up north and west. His dad was proud, man. He was unshakable. Those dudes would get right in the old man's face and he'd just stand there. Wouldn't blink. I'm older then R, and I was a teen then. I remember seeing that shit and thinking, 'this old man...' He was the last holdout. Then one night, middle of the night, they burned the place down, blocked the doors with trash cans. I remember seeing it go down. The old man burned up, so did R's sister, Kathleen. Burned up his arm a little, too, but he got out."

Melissa had stopped crying. She stared straight ahead, completely entranced in the narrative unfolding over the phone. She could barely believe her ears—it sounded like the plot of a film.

Luis continued, "We stayed tight. He's a weird guy, you know that. But he gets it. So, we been taking the town back. He moved uptown to avoid suspicion. And we been taking them out. Piece by piece. Piece of shit by piece of shit. R uses fire, explosives. Says it's poetic. They took his family out with fire and he'll bring it back to rain on them. Fire for evil, fire for good." Luis laughed. Melissa did not.

She spoke up. "We?"

"R really. I help out. So does my brother. We believe in the cause. A lot of us do. He's a hero down here. Like a superhero. The kids literally talk about the weird guy who never leaves his house except to take out the bad guys."

"So who is setting all the other fires?"

More silence. Finally, "I don't know. None of us do."

Melissa's voice suddenly became louder, as though she suddenly had a thought that she couldn't bare for Luis to miss. "Do me a favor."

"Sure?" Luis seemed taken aback by the sudden change.

"Tell Roman that it wasn't me. I didn't tell anyone about his basement. I mean, no cops, no firefighters. Nothing like that. I don't know how they know. Please tell him."

Luis' voice sounded more soothing and paternal than ever, and he said "I will" with a conviction and honesty that couldn't be doubted. Melissa's shoulders relaxed and she slumped back onto the couch a bit.

Luis continued, "But it'll be a waste of time. Because we know who called in the tip."

Melissa was confused. She started to ask a question, but didn't know what to ask. A strange, breathy crackle escaped from her throat. Luis didn't let her suffer. "We called it in. The firebug doing the bad shit has someone to take the fall. He gets a free pass. So we call it in, one of two things happens. Scenario one, R takes the whole fall, and innocent people stop getting hurt. The firebug takes the free pass and moves on. Scenario two, the guy continues. Maybe R gets a lessened sentence. But it's a risk we needed to take. We started this, and now innocent people are getting hurt from a copycat or whatever. Can't have it."

90

Silence.

Luis spoke up. "I should go."

Melissa sighed and rubbed her eyes. "Yeah. Thank you. One more thing."

"Yeah?"

"Why are you doing this? Just because you believe it's right?"

"R saved my life once. Really saved it." He paused. "And he shouldn't have. And I'm forever in his debt."

"Wait."

"Yeah?"

"Why are you calling me? Why are you telling me all this?"

"R asked me to. You're going to want that information. You're going to help us out pretty soon." With this, he hung up.

# 29

Melissa stared at the phone in her hand, shock keeping her from processing all the information that now ran through her mind. Roman was guilty, that was confirmed. But only...half? It didn't make any sense, but at the same time, relief began to settle in her stomach, the knots that formed after that first discovery in his basement untying for the first time since then. Tears crept to the corner of her eyes and paused, waiting to see if they should be of joy or dread.

She unlocked her phone and pulled up her contact list, carefully dragging the screen down with her index finger until she saw Roman's information. She clicked on it, extending his profile. She found herself staring at a picture of him looking off into the distance that she had quietly taken when he wasn't looking at her. She couldn't help but smile at his intensity, but a nagging thought began to tug at the back of her mind. Was that otherworldly focus one of the traits of someone who was a pyromaniac? It was a sobering thought that crashed into her chest like a punch. Regardless of how innocent he may be, he was still someone that played with fire, quite possibly even getting off on it. No matter how much she cared for him—every time he struck a match, every time he lit a candle—would she be able to truly trust him?

Oh my god, she loved him.

The tears received her command: dread. They began to trickle down her cheeks, cascading down her face like messengers, warning of a larger storm to come. She put the phone down and began to pace the room. She hated having these thoughts. Anyone else would have felt relief that they had been spared from a possible death; he is not completely innocent. But he was Roman. Every weird quirk and odd turn of phrase felt so much more genuine than anything she had experienced since...forever. He was only half guilty. But half guilty did not translate to half a firebug. This...affliction...would always be a part of him and something she would have to deal with in one way or another.

Right?

Robin Hood worked well in a Disney movie, but the reality was much harsher than fiction can sometimes allow. If Luis was right, then Roman had a reason for what he did; a good one perhaps, though logic dictated there were much better ways of dealing with it. But this band of merry men that were helping Roman legitimately scared her; they may not be as knowledgeable as

Roman, or even have the moral compass required to justify such actions. Every fire they set had real world ramifications. Were there any homeless people in those buildings? What would happen if the wind blew west instead of east, lighting up another building next door? One that might have tenants. Would they have even cared?

Half guilty.

These were all sound, logical thoughts that a sane, logical person should have. Unfortunately, Melissa wasn't in an entirely logical state of mind at the moment. She would find a way to rationalize loving Roman, even if it meant lying to herself in some way. She knew there was no way to change him. This is what he is. But maybe, just maybe, they could find a way to make it work.

The only problem, of course, was finding the other arsonist. And that whole prison thing.

# 30

Melissa found herself sitting on the couch again, her chest on her thighs, folded and looking down at piles of research that lay scattered on the carpet.

If Roman had only set the drug house fires, who had set the rest? Was it a coincidence? A copycat? Was there a motive? Or was it sheer, unadulterated pyromania? Was Luis telling the truth? Was Roman telling the truth?

She shook her head. The questions came tumbling over one another, falling into a maddening heap of multisensory commotion.

She stood and paced back and forth, looking down at the research she had gathered, but seeing nothing in particular. Hospitals. Malls. Retirement communities. Medical centers. What's the connection? Large groups of people in one place—in one large structure? People who aren't perfectly mobile and therefore can't escape? No, that doesn't make sense for the malls or medical centers, only the hospitals and retirement communities.

Was it death that the second arsonist sought? None of the fires were significant, and the only death arose out of sheer happenstance.

Hospitals. Malls. Retirement communities. Medical centers. Hospitals. Malls...

She froze in her tracks, as though moving would frighten her thought away like a deer. She held her breath and stared into space. She dove to her knees, and tore through the mounds of loosely-grouped papers and enlarged photographs, searching for actual snapshots of each scene. Mall. Hospital. Mall again. Medical center. Hospital. She was throwing research aside with her right hand, and clutching her findings to her breast with her left, crouching like a gargoyle.

Many fires occurred at night, when no one was around, and those during the day—she continued digging—the hospital fires were all in secure areas next to loading docks. The retirement community fire was in a secure storage area adjacent to a hallway with access to a kitchen.

Secure areas.

Melissa scrambled through the photographs for shots from outside the areas where the fires had originated. Most of the shots' angles failed to provide her with what she was looking for. And then, in one of the hospital photos, she found it. The photograph was from the inside of a loading dock, showing the wall that had been burned through. On the other side of the wall, through the charred remains of a 2 x 4 frame, one could see the room where the fire had started. In the very top-right section of the photograph, just barely within the frame, was a keyless entry sensor.

Her face and hands went cold, and she was transported back to her first date with Shaun. Intoxicated with a cocktail of emotions, the vision came to her with a clarity and realism that she had never before experienced; she smelled the musky bouquet of the alley, felt Shaun's pulse pump through her left hand. She felt the newness of their love and the crisp air brushing against her thin cotton skirt.

*"Key to the city,"* he had said, swiping his magnetic key against a black square and watching the tiny red light turn green. *"Everything is ten years behind here, they don't track anything."*

# 31

Melissa peeled out of her parking space, her left hand on the steering wheel, her right hand clutching her phone. The other line was silent for a moment.

"That's a fairly giant leap you're taking, sis." Terry said, breaking the silence. "Are you really sure that's an accusation you want to make?"

Melissa hesitated before she answered. She wasn't sure at all, but her journalistic gut was pounding away. "It's...circumstantial. Hold on a sec."

Melissa pulled up to a stop light. She removed the phone from her ear, set it to speaker, and dropped it on her lap. She needed to focus, not crash her car. She took both hands and dug into the steering wheel's rubbery plastic, the slight burn on her fingers taking the place of the guttural scream that she desperately needed to release.

"You still there?"

Melissa took a deep breath before answering. "I don't know what to do. What do I do?" It wasn't a question she expected to hear an answer to; she just needed to say it out loud.

"Can you go to the police?"

Melissa shook her head, and then verbalized the response. "And tell them what? I'm not even sure I'm right. I could be in the middle of a complete breakdown for all I know!"

"Talk to him."

Melissa stared forward. "What?"

"Call him. Ask him. Confront him." Terry said, with a matter-of-factness that took Melissa by surprise. "For some incredibly fucked-up reason, you love the other pyro, right?"

The absurdity of the statement hit Melissa like a ton of bricks. What the hell had she gotten herself into?

"I do, yes. I know it's...I can't explain it."

"Right. So Shaun's out of the picture. What the hell do you care if you hurt his feelings? Worst case, you know he's not the other arsonist and you end up doing your job. You go report."

Melissa hadn't told Terry that she had gotten back together with Shaun. Did she care if she hurt his feelings? She couldn't tell. She pulled over to the side of the road. Terry was making sense. What was the worst that could happen? He could hurt her—or worse—but was that really a risk? This wasn't a movie.

"Thank you", Melissa said, as she put the car in reverse. "You're right. I need to talk to him."

She could hear Terry smile through the phone. "How much bullshit have I put you through? Least I could do was help you the one time you actually need it."

Melissa picked the phone back up and cradled it against her ear. "I need you to do me a favor."

"Anything."

"Keep this to yourself for now. I'm going to give him a call. I'll talk to you in a bit."

"Good luck," Terry said. As she was about to hang up the phone, Melissa stopped her. "Hey!"

"Yes?" Terry asked.

"Remember when you said you wished something exciting would happen?"

Terry laughed. "Yeah."

"Looks like you got your wish."

Melissa tossed her phone on the passenger seat and braced herself. This wasn't a conversation that should happen by phone. She needed to do this in person.

# 32

Melissa had calmed herself down on the drive to Shaun's house. She had no idea if he was home; he could be working or out running errands. She convinced herself that it couldn't have been Shaun who set those fires; he was a man sworn to protect the city and prevent the very phenomenon that she thought he was causing. What would be his motive? Should she call the cops?

Bennett? She realized that her heart was racing again and focused on slowing her breathing.

It was as though fate had rolled out a red carpet for Melissa that night: the weather was beautiful, she found a parking spot directly outside Shaun's house, and—as she could tell from the lights in the living room—Shaun was home. She walked up to the front door and rang the bell.

Until now, she was too preoccupied with emotions and confusion to consider how she would approach the delicate subject matter. As footsteps approached the door, she bounced back and forth between being embarrassed for even considering that Shaun may be the arsonist and being so sure of it that she was afraid of how he may react to being discovered.

The door opened, just as she was transitioning from embarrassment to anger. She decided to opt for an opener that could catch Shaun off guard and thus expose him.

"I know everything," Melissa said before the door was even entirely open. Shaun could immediately see that she was dead serious and armed with more than a hunch. He attempted no poker face and awaited her reasoning without expression.

She continued confidently, adjusting her posture a bit to give off an air of dignity as would a little girl. "I know about the fires. I know how you were getting into those areas. I know—"

She cut herself off, realizing that she didn't know anything else. His face was one of terror. "I know—" she started again. She exhaled, relaxed her spine, and let her hands fall to her sides with an audible clap of defeat. "I just don't know *why*. Why would you do that?"

Without uttering a word, Shaun stepped back from the entryway, creating a passage between Melissa and the couch. She took a few tentative steps into the home and turned toward him. His eyes were pointed dully at the ground in front of his feet. She continued to the couch and sat down. He sat down in a matching chair across from her, leaned forward, and rested his elbows on his knees. His fingers were loosely intertwined, and touched his thumbs together, as though he were matching their prints.

"There's no...crazy reason," he began. "It's simple. It's...utilitarian." His eyes were fixed on Melissa's feet, her eyes on his mouth. Melissa felt as though she were sinking into another world; her lip began to quiver and her eyes began to tear with disgust. Until this moment, it had only been suspicion. This can't really be happening. Shaun couldn't really have been the arsonist. Could he? Shaun continued, breaking Melissa from her trance.

"It was really just job security. Fires equal work. I'm not the only one. Bennigan and Waine were doing it too. We were all doing it together."

Her silence was deafening.

"Not that that makes it better," he said, relaxing somewhat into his seat. "I mean, it wasn't to be a hero. It wasn't to...it was literally just to keep the bell ringing down at the station. To put money in our wallets. No fires, more cutbacks, less firefighters." The tone of the last word rose a bit, as though he was setting it up for some sort of impending resolution. He looked straight at Melissa, and finished. "Money for us. For our future. For the life I thought we'd have together. One I thought we lost, but lately..." He sat forward and reached for her hand; the motion in no way reflected the sincerity of his words, but rather came across as a desperate, clawing action. She recoiled.

Melissa was unable to string together a coherent thought, and Shaun just stared at her. He seemed to be on the verge of tears. Melissa felt no sympathy, no connection, no hatred, no judgment. She felt nothing. She resented the fact that he had brought her to this state. She resented that he was able to turn her into an unfeeling shell, capable of staring into the eyes of someone she was supposed to love without feeling a single emotion.

Finally, three words squeaked past her lips. They were confident and restrained, half whispered and half spoken, like the well-thought-out final words of a dying woman.

"You're a monster."

Melissa calmly moved to leave, but suddenly became afraid. She stopped and looked at Shaun, fully expecting him to try to stop her. Here stood the one person who knew his secret; would he let her leave? As she stepped toward the door, she watched him. He simply stared at the ground between them as she walked out the door. Whether due to shame, shock, or resignation, Shaun had just given her license to leave with this massive piece of information in tow.

Melissa began to drive. She had no idea where she was going. Her phone buzzed incessantly as Shaun tried to reach her. Finally, she picked up. Without allowing Shaun to utter a single word, she exploded.

"Let me tell you something, she said." She pulled the car over, shaking uncontrollably.

"My whole fucking life. You. Terry. Mom. The paper. All these other shitty, boring guys from my past. My career. Like...I just spend all this time doing what's right. Or trying to do what's right. Or even pretending to do what's right..." Her speech was frantic. She was almost screaming, and speaking so quickly that Shaun could hardly understand her. She was pounding the steering wheel with her right palm. "Or pretending to *try* to do what's right."

She stopped for a minute to take a breath. "Fuck what's right. I'm doing something that *feels* right. Even though it's obviously completely fucking wrong. The guy is a headcase, Shaun." She went on, paying no attention to the fact that she was now speaking about Roman, about whom Shaun knew nothing. "I know this. He knows this. And now maybe I am too, but I don't care. A headcase. I *want* wrong. I want him to fill me with his wrongness. I want to be one of his buildings, I want him to destroy me, burn me down. Relieve me of this dreadful feeling that I'm supposed to have structure."

Silence. Shaun must have been more confused than he'd been in a very long time.

"Shaun, you're destroying your buildings. He's freeing his from housing all that pain and hatred. You're destroying lives. He's doing battle against everything that's soulless and evil." With that, Melissa hung up the phone and cried intensely for a few minutes with her forehead on the steering wheel. Shaun called back about ten minutes later, and Melissa reluctantly picked up. She said nothing. After a moment, Shaun spoke quietly.

"Are you going to the cops?"

"Yes." She wasn't. She didn't know if the cops would protect her, but she knew Roman would, if she could somehow get to him. Shaun hadn't mentioned the rant that she had just delivered.

"If you do that, you know what I'm going to have to do, right?"

Melissa's heart froze. Shaun continued.

"I loved you, but if you're gone, and it's you or me, I choose me. So that's the deal. You live your life, I live mine, all is fine and dandy. You go to someone about this—anyone-—and the deal is off. You broke the trust. And I'll take you with me to whatever hell I end up in."

Melissa was shaking uncontrollably.

"You want a monster?" Shaun asked, his voice intense and filtered through his teeth, "I'll show you a monster."

# 33

Melissa sat across from Roman, separated by a long piece of bulletproof glass, a telephone receiver dangling from either side of it. She placed her tape recorder on the small ledge that helped keep the glass in place. She bit the corner of her cheek to keep herself in check as she slowly raised her head to make eye contact with Roman. Remember, she thought to herself, you don't know him. You're doing your job. Stay professional. Her eyes finally settled on his.

A small smirk lay on the left cleft of his lip as he reached for the phone.

"Good day, miss."

Melissa held her breath before she spoke. She needed to stay in character.

"Do you know who I am?" she asked.

Roman tapped on the glass. "Judging by the incredibly old tape recorder you're holding to that phone, I'd deduce that you're a reporter for a rapidly declining news outlet."

"Correct."

"I certainly hope these questions get harder."

Roman, always pushing buttons. Always testing her. She wanted to laugh and strangle him all in one thought.

"Tell this reporter for a declining news outlet why you did what you did."

"I tried to get in touch with someone at the paper a little bit ago. Waited for them at a diner for hours. No one showed." He smiled. "She was pretty though, so I just watched her eat some pie."

Melissa blushed. She would normally have been massively creeped out, but given Roman's style, she found herself flattered and slightly turned on.

Roman leaned back in his chair, the slack on the phone's cord tugging on its receiver, straightening out its rubber coils, tensing like the air that carried the question.

"So why did I do it? Easy. I didn't." He paused for a second. "Well, the not all the ones they're charging me for. I was responsible for the houses, but no hospitals. No malls. Not my M.O. Morally vapid business, that is."

She looked at him, puzzled. Why was he confessing to her?

"What is your M.O. then?"

Roman pointed to a police officer who sat in the corner, struggling with a Sudoku puzzle.

"Ask him. A shrink came in. I'm sure it's on file somewhere. They think I'm sociopathic. Or autistic. Some unlikely marriage of the two, perhaps. Mainly because I chose all the fun answers. Laughed at their pseudoscience."

Melissa had to keep her jaw from dropping. What was his game?

"They're taking me uptown later today, I'd assume, to one of the two bigger stations," he continued. "It'd make for a better story, I think, if you

103

found out details about that transfer. The whens and wheres. The devil is in the details, you know."

She cocked her head.

He sensed her confusion and spoke a bit more slowly and deliberately. "You really should find out when and where they're transferring me. It would make for a great story." Then he snapped his fingers and again began speaking at his normal pace. "Hey, I have this childhood friend, Luis. Great grasp of the English language. A poet at heart. He could edit the piece for you when you're done. You know, spell check, make sure you're not overusing semicolons, those types of things."

A small smile crept upon his face as he tapped his finger against his left temple. As though to poke fun at the fact that the officer was paying no attention whatsoever, Roman loudly added, "Wink. Nudge."

She covered her mouth, and nodded, letting him know she understood. As deep in this whole mess as she had become—having been intimate with both arsonists—this was something different. This was an actual crime they were talking about.

Melissa pushed back her chair and motioned to the officer. He didn't look up.

"Officer?" she said. His head snapped up.

"I'm not getting anything here. Thanks for letting me in, but this nutjob's talking crazy."

She turned off her recorder and made her way to the door. On her way out, she asked the officer if there was anyone she should speak with to get more details about the case.

# 34

Hours later, Melissa sat in her car, her fingers nervously dancing upon her steering wheel. The sun had started to set, casting ominous shadows over the row homes and corner shops, heightening the drama of the situation that Melissa had already began to exaggerate in her mind. It all felt like a dream. She peered down at the clock on the car's radio to find that the time hadn't changed since she had last checked just moments earlier. Frustrated, she switched her rhythmless beat from the wheel to her car's dashboard, ending it with an open-handed slap. She unbuckled her seatbelt and threw open the door.

She thought back to the conversation with Luis that had had occurred two hours prior. After she relayed the necessary information, he went silent for a minute. She could hear him fumbling with something, perhaps a pencil and paper. Finally, he had said "Thanks for the call. By the way, right along that route, there's an awesome little torta shop. It's on the corner of Ivy and 8th. If I remember correctly, R loves it. I don't suppose the cops driving him from station to station would be kind enough to stop for him, do you?"

"I don't." She said, not understanding his implication at the time.

"That's a shame. They make a mean torta. You should try it. They have a special at 4:30 today."

A barking dog brought her back into the present. Melissa surveyed the area, not sure what it was she should be looking for. What had he planned? She saw no shadowy figures hiding in dark alleyways. No curtains pulled back, beady eyes peering out upon the street. There weren't even any children playing soccer or baseball, ready to yell when the five-oh would turn the

105

corner. The torta shop was the least shady of all. It was boring, with a generic green sign and a black and white printed menu. She considered for a moment that this could all be some cruel joke.

That's when she saw the light.

It was a quick flash at first, a blinking red light reflecting off the window of a shutdown bodega. Melissa hesitantly made her way down the street, clenching a fist around her car keys, the teeth of which rested between her middle and index finger; a makeshift weapon to keep her safe. As she approached, the red light grew larger but remained unmoving, like a lighthouse beacon warning of an upcoming shoreline. She paused and took a deep breath, the adrenaline pumping through her body. She became hyperconscious of her clothing, the light wind on her cheeks. This was it. She turned the corner.

A crowd of people had swarmed a police car. Makeshift roadblocks comprised of rundown Ford pickups and minivans blocked both sides of the street. Groups of people peppered the street, laughing and talking excitedly in Spanish. Melissa slowly approached the mob scene. As everything became focused, she noticed something to her left: two police officers, terror on their faces, swaddled in blankets with obese men sitting on each. The sight was nightmarish and absurd. Melissa stumbled with light-headedness. Was this real?

"Remarkable what reciprocity will get you, is it not?"

Melissa jumped and turned around. She faced Roman.

He smirked in that way she just couldn't resist. Suddenly overcome with emotion, Melissa greeted him with a kiss. She pulled away and looked up, tears welling in her eyes. She loved him. Her life changed in that moment.

"Where do we go from here?" she asked.

"We need to make a statement," Roman said. When Melissa looked over at the overtaken police car, he continued. "A statement bigger than that."

Melissa smiled at him. Roman returned it. In an instant, Melissa pieced together Roman's intention. The fact that she could even think of such a thing was proof that there was no going back.

# 35

The first alarm sounded at 9:26PM, with the first truck responding by 9:29. It was a one-alarmer a mile away from the station, an abandoned row house where some homeless schmuck had fallen asleep and let a small trash can fire get quickly out of control. While the fire was surely containable, it would take some time to be extinguished. The firehouse was now down to two engines.

The second alarm sounded at 9:42PM, with the second engine responding by 9:44. It was a three alarmer in the next county over, a warehouse fire. A presumed drunk driver had plowed into a telephone pole, knocking the wooden sentinel into the side of the building, severing a power line that lit the weather worn roof up like kindling. It was looking to be an all-nighter on that one. The Washington Valley No. 1 Fire Company was now down to one solitary engine.

The final alarm sounded at 10:08PM, with the last engine responding by 10:12. Civil unrest had erupted earlier in the night, at the corner of eighth and Ivy, when a few residents had jumped a police car and assisted in the escape of a known felon. Order had seemed to be restored, until a Molotov cocktail shattered the window of a Mexican sandwich shop. The building was quickly enveloped in flames, assisted by the grease that had been stored precariously on the countertop. Residents were now starting another commotion, so the estimated time of the engine's return was to be determined.

Sgt. Smith watched the last engine drive away. He was now the only firefighter left at the station. He paced about in galoshes, ready to jump into the fire marshal's SUV if he was needed at any of the three active zones. He picked a cup of coffee up off a workman's table as he closed the firehouse's garage doors and made his way up to the kitchen, where he pulled a pot from a side cabinet and placed it in the sink to fill it with tap water. As he turned, prepared to access the fridge, an unknown fist connected with his jaw. Before Sgt. Smith blacked out, he briefly saw a silhouette of his assailant, a heavyset Latino man.

# 36

A block away, in a black, nondescript car, Melissa's phone rang, breaking the silence. She handed it to Roman, who picked it up. His escape— the drama, fire, and mobs of people—all seemed distant now.

"It's done," Luis' voice said, before hanging up.

Roman smiled and returned the phone to his pocket, before turning to Melissa, who sat in the passenger seat. He moved his right hand to her left thigh and began to stroke her leg.

"Are you ready?" he asked, as he leaned in to kiss her neck. The slow, deliberate gesture seemed outwardly sweet, but really served to drag out the inevitable.

Melissa took her left hand and rubbed Roman's right thigh, making sure to playfully brush the growing bulge in his pants. Two could play at this game.

"Let's do it." she said.

Roman put his hand on the gear shift and turned to Melissa. "Last chance to live a restful girl scout life. Is the lady certain that she wishes to go through with this?"

Melissa's silence provided a foundation for the determination beaming from her eyes. Roman nodded and put the car into drive. It was time.

# 37

"Found it."

With an echoey click, Roman flipped a switch and turned on the lights. They came on one at a time, about a quarter of a second apart from each other, traveling away from them.

Melissa looked around, surprised at the realization that—despite all the time she'd spent with Shaun—she'd never been to the fire station before this night.

"So, how do we do this?" she asked. Roman didn't respond, and when Melissa turned to find him, she saw that he was already a few steps away, looking at the building's 200-volt electrical service box. He popped it open, and ran his finger down the fuses. At first Melissa thought that he was quickly reading the label on each, but then she realized that his eyes were shut, and that he was simply relishing the feel of the plastic—the power he wielded and the significance of what he was about to do. He was exhaling slowly.

He calmly turned to her and smiled. "I know what to do. Are you sure you're ready to do this?"

She swallowed loudly and nodded. After realizing that the nod was a bit timid and thinking about how unsure the gesture seemed, she followed it with a much louder, "I'm ready." He turned back to the service box and busied his hands for a few moments. Melissa felt her body relax as she watched his fingers work and thought about how they'd be working on her shortly. The thought filled her with a warmth that began low, as though she were a bathtub quickly filling with water.

After introducing some balled up paper to the wires that he had twisted, he stepped away and turned to her.

Melissa walked up and kissed him quickly and gently. She pulled about an inch away, and hesitated. Their eyes opened and locked for a moment, and she kissed him again; this kiss was much more passionate, and she reached up behind his head and pulled him close to her.

Her right hand came to rest on his chest, and slid down to his stomach. She turned her hand so that her fingers faced downward, letting her fingertips slide slowly down his muscular torso. She could feel tension in his body as he shuddered.

Melissa undid Roman's belt and slid it out of the loops that held it in place. She was about to place it on the table next to them, but then began to see the first signs of smoke rising from behind him, reminding her how futile it would be to place the belt anywhere with any care; instead, she let it drop to the ground. The quick, dull, percussive sound of the buckle hitting the concrete was like a bell that set Roman off, and he suddenly pressed his groin into hers, pulling her hips into his as though he were trying to wrap himself in her. She felt tension and warmth pulsing through his pants, like a barking, enraged animal being held against its will behind a closed door.

Melissa unzipped Roman's pants, and knelt to slide them off. Face to face with his boxer-briefs, the heat and curve of his stifled manhood pulsed at her, and she became aware of a subtle-yet-beautiful duality; while Roman's manhood seemed impatient and carnal, the man who wielded it seemed completely composed. More than composed, really—he seemed serene. He looked to be savoring the moment, allowing anticipation to hold him like a lover. Melissa went from kneeling stiffly to relaxing onto her calves, with half of her behind resting on the ground. Gripping the hips of his underwear with her thumbs, she slowly lowered them, exposing him inch by raging inch. Though they had made love in the light before, she had never seen him in this way; the fluorescent lights made everything seem like a film. As the last of his manhood was unleashed from its cruel captor, it burst upward. From her position on the ground, she looked up at him.

Light bulbs began to burst in the background.

Melissa slowly took Roman into her mouth. He inhaled deeply, shut his eyes, and leaned back onto a stool. Melissa's thighs tingled, and a heat traveled up into her body, into her stomach, into her chest. She shut her eyes and took him in and out with an increasing intensity. She felt as though he was not inside her mouth, but rather down below; she could feel him quiver as she pulled him deeper and deeper into her. Her lips tickled at the touch of his skin; he was soft and smooth, yet taut, as though the skin was the only thing protecting the world from the animal hidden in his throbbing flesh. Her right hand found its way up his leg and began to assist her rhythm.

She opened her eyes. Flames were all around them, and the ceiling was obscured by a dense layer of smoke. Melissa froze, terrified for a brief moment, her heart offering one single, loud, shocking beat as though she had been struck.

When she calmed down, she was surprised to find that the fingers of her free hand had found their way between her legs, and that they had been dancing in rhythm with the pleasure that she bestowed upon her lover.

Broken out of his daze by the pause, Roman opened his eyes to find the ceiling beginning to catch flame. He looked down, ran his fingers down Melissa's face, and, for a brief moment, they were hypnotized by the reflection of orange flame dancing within each other's eyes. He helped her up, hoisted her onto a desk, and slid her panties off. Beginning with her left knee, he slowly kissed his way up toward her, and began to return the favor. He was a master of anticipation.

Almost immediately upon his arriving at his final destination, Melissa's breath and heart began to quicken. She felt her eyes well up with tears, as she felt Roman's gentle breath against her thighs in between his tender, slow kisses. His tongue danced a ballet of ecstasy.

Melissa shut her eyes and looked up. The flames were all around them at this point, and she could hear the roar of flames begin to crescendo. This sound was punctuated by the occasional crash of breaking glass or bang of an object falling from a dissolving wooden table. The smell became stronger, and she found herself momentarily distracted by the commotion, until she suddenly felt Roman slide into her.

He did so slowly and uniformly; a ten-second, exquisite connection that filled her with sensations so precise and intimate that she was sure she'd be able to remember the details forever. She felt every detail—every ridge, every contour—of his manhood as the two became one. When he was completely inside her, his warm body pressed up against her, she reached for his hand. He gave it willingly, and they kissed as the building around them began to erupt at an ever-quickening pace.

It was eleven PM. As the large electric clock above them buzzed, Roman was falling into Melissa with a ferocious intensity, his hands gripping her backside, and each thrust bringing Melissa a staccato flash of ecstasy. A loud crash came from behind them, near the entrance to the hallway they had barricaded.

They were surrounded by bright yellow, screaming flames; more importantly, they were surrounded by the entirety of the city's firefighting supplies. They were untouchable.

The heat was overbearing, and their lungs began to burn. The small pieces of plaster that had been falling around them gave way to somewhat larger, structural pieces of the ceiling. His grip on her behind tightened, causing her pain that mixed perfectly with both the pleasure being unleashed inside her and the unbearable heat of the fire that now almost engulfed them.

Melissa stared up at Roman, hoping to meet his eyes. She instead found them fixed straight ahead, his neck tight with an inhuman tension. He looked to be screaming, but she could hear nothing but the roar of the flames. Melissa could feel him release into her, his body becoming a surreal, rigid statue. Red from the flames, covered in sweat, with a crazed expression, Roman looked like the devil. He was laughing, crying, screaming. The muscles of his hard stomach tightened as though they were making a fist within him. Melissa was so close, her breath quickening, her loud moans hushed by the chorus of churning flames.

That's when she saw him. Shaun was standing in the doorway. Melissa froze, unable to process what she was seeing. She looked past him to see that he had kicked through the barricade, assumedly to do his duty as a firefighter, and had no idea that he might walk in on his ex-girlfriend making love to a stranger. His face was one of pure, stereotypical astonishment, his mouth agape, and both hands placed atop his head.

Without seeing Shaun, Roman slowly slid out of her, a few brief moments that felt like a lifetime of pleasure. Just then, Shaun suddenly seemed to snap out of it and walk toward them. Roman saw him out of the corner of his eye just in time to sidestep a punch thrown by Shaun. Roman came up and instinctively tackled Shaun, pinning him against a shelving unit full of equipment. Helmets and facemasks fell silently to the ground, a true testament to the sheer volume of sound generated by the flames.

Melissa was about to stand, but began to black out when she tried. The mixture of heat and pleasure eased her back onto the table. Her right hand touched her face, finding it drenched in sweat. Her loins continued to throb, and she let her hand lazily slide down between her legs. She found her place, shut her eyes, and lost herself in the flames.

With tears of pain, joy, terror, and ecstasy pouring down her face, Melissa came. Her vision faded, and the obnoxious sounds of the room became distant. Lost in a tense orgasm that felt as though her very soul were being squeezed from all sides, she surrendered all to this man, to this place, to this decision. She surrendered the past year, the indiscretions, the decisions, and gave herself wholly to the merciless and cleansing flame.

At 1:18AM, surrounded by a crowd of awestruck bystanders and helpless plainclothes firefighters, the Washington Valley No. 1 Fire Company collapsed to the ground, lighting the surrounding city as a flurry of bright ash was cast into the deep purple summer sky.

# 38

*Only one body has been found so far in the smoldering remains of what was once the historic Washington Valley Fire Department. The victim has been identified as firefighter Shaun Duchane. It was believed that the remains of Roman Carver, the Washington Valley Firebug who allegedly caused the fire, would eventually be located within the sprawling cinders. Duchane's girlfriend, Melissa Blume, is also missing. A manhunt is being organized, but no action will be taken until police determine what role she may have played in this bizarre story. Was she a victim or co-conspirator? More information would come shortly, updates at every seven on the hour.*

Terry smiled as she leaned into her car and switched off the radio, thus ending the misinformation that spouted through her car's tinny speakers. She knew the real story, the facts left out of the report. The bodies weren't found because the bodies weren't there. In fact, they were in her eye line, specks in the distance loading supplies into a small boat in a small town somewhere on the central Jersey shoreline. The report also failed to mention that Roman's car was no longer in the impound lot, the fence cut with the obvious tools and skill of an amateur. But most importantly, she knew the truth. A stack of

115

evidence proving that several firefighters were involved in the recent arson spree was helpfully left for the police in the exact spot where Roman's car had sat, literally topped with a red Christmas bow. Curiously, nothing seemed to come about from this evidence. The radio told the truth that the town needed to hear; the real truth remained with those who needed to know it.

As she watched her sister interacting with Roman, a slight knot began to tie in her stomach; a fear she was afraid to speak out loud for fear of taking the smile off her sister's beaming face.

Shaun was a man tainted with an immoral selfishness that couldn't be forgiven. But Roman was plagued with something potentially worse: a mysterious, formless darkness. Something in his eyes. Unlike Shaun, who used fire in a—to quote him—utilitarian sense, Roman may have actually had a bit of a firebug within him. He was stable—at least that's what Melissa said, though Terry barely believed it—but how long would this stability last in the face of all the recent happenings? And what would they do? Live on a boat? Sail from port to port? Terry knew the duo had a plan, but really, this was as far along as they had really thought it through. The rest would be the true adventure.

Terry was distracted from her thoughts as her sister's waving arms brought her back to reality. The boat was slowly making its way from the shore. Terry quickly stepped up onto the hood of her car and returned the wave, following it up with an exaggerated blown kiss, her hand kept on her mouth for an extra few seconds to showcase her joy. Melissa responded with a pantomime hug, and then turned to help Roman with some nautical task.

Terry sat down on the roof of her car and watched as the two sailed off, unsure of where they would end up. Where she would end up. But it didn't matter. Roman had freed the two of them from the burden of their own fear, just as he had freed the buildings from the burden of their own structure. Through destruction they had all been made whole.

Made in the USA
Charleston, SC
14 December 2012